I0838205

Cinnamon, Lies, and Ledgers

A Story of Secrets, Silence, and the Search for Justice

Tumblebrook Mysteries
Book 4

Ellen Le Teace

Bradford
Press

Copyright © 2025 by Bradford Press

All rights reserved.

No part of this book may be reproduced in any form or by any electronic or mechanical means, including information storage and retrieval systems, without written permission from the author, except for the use of brief quotations in a book review.

 Formatted with Vellum

Chapter 1

The Haunting of Tumblebrook Inn

The wind had teeth. It shrieked through the hills, clawing at the corners of Tumblebrook Inn like a caged animal. The inn — a sturdy, three-story structure that had withstood decades of northern Minnesota storms — creaked beneath the onslaught as if it, too, felt the storm's fury. Trees bowed under the wind's weight, and the lake, visible through the rain-streaked windows, churned with restless waves.

Inside, Amelia Farnsworth tightened the belt of her cardigan and adjusted her grip on the guestbook. The comforting scent of cinnamon tea lingered in the air, mingling with the earthy aroma of wood smoke from the hearth. Despite the inn's warmth, unease clung to the air like a stubborn chill.

She moved to the front window, eyes fixed on the gravel driveway. Headlights pierced the downpour, inching along the winding path. Her final guest for the night had arrived. The car rolled to a stop, and a man emerged, hunched against the wind, dragging a suitcase and a newspaper-wrapped bundle. His coat flapped wildly, his hat nearly torn from his head.

Amelia had just set the kettle to boil when the front door burst open, bringing a rush of cold air and the scent of wet pine. "Mr. Maddox!" she called, stepping forward with a welcoming smile.

The man, tall and wiry, shook rain from his coat and removed his fogged glasses. His skin was pale, his eyes tired behind wire-rimmed frames.

"Ms. Farnsworth," he said warmly. "Thanks for keeping the light on."

"Always," Amelia replied, handing him a towel. "Let me take that for you. Room five, just as before."

Together, they ascended the staircase, each step groaning beneath their weight. The inn was old, but it had character — the kind that wrapped around visitors like a warm quilt. Lady Grey, Amelia's British Shorthair, perched on the landing, amber eyes fixed on Mr. Maddox. She didn't move. Didn't purr. Just watched.

"She remembers you," Amelia said lightly, though her brow furrowed. Lady Grey was many things — curious, quirky, and occasionally mischievous — but rarely still.

Once Mr. Maddox was settled with a blanket and tea, Amelia lingered outside the door, listening. His voice, muffled by the wood, was low and urgent. One phrase stood out: "It's not safe here."

Amelia shivered and made her way downstairs. The rain hadn't let up — if anything, it intensified, hammering the windows with relentless fury. She carried her tea to the parlor and sank into her favorite armchair, cushions worn to her shape. But she couldn't relax. Lady Grey sat at her feet, fur bristling, gaze fixed on the basement door.

"What is it?" Amelia asked. The cat chirped, padded to the door, and scratched.

"Now?" Amelia sighed, setting her cup aside. "Fine. Let's see what's so important."

The basement was the inn's memory box — forgotten linens, a rocking chair with a splintered leg, a portrait of the original owners. The air was thick with mildew and old secrets. Amelia switched on the flashlight, its beam sweeping across the clutter.

Lady Grey trotted ahead, tail high, weaving through crates. She stopped in the far corner where a crooked bookshelf leaned against the stone wall. The flashlight caught gold lettering on a faded leather spine. Amelia crouched, brushing away cobwebs. One wall panel felt loose.

"What did you find?" she murmured. She pressed the plank. It slid aside with a soft scrape, revealing a hidden compartment.

Inside: a rusted tin box and a leather-bound journal. The name stamped into the cracked cover sent a jolt through her.

Annie Farnsworth.

Her great-aunt. Annie had run the inn in its early days — a collector of folk tales, a scribbler of marginalia, a woman who spoke of "Watchers" and vanished one summer without a trace. Some said she went mad. Others said she saw too much.

Amelia opened the journal. The pages crackled, ink faded but readable. Dated entries from the late 1950s, written in a looping, frantic hand.

"Saw them again tonight," one entry read. "Behind the bakery, whispering. Martin looked scared. He said they knew. They always know."

"The Watcher," another entry read, underlined three times. "By the lake. Watching the water. Watching me. Watching everything."

Amelia's pulse quickened. She'd heard the name — whispered by old-timers at the café, always with unease. The Watcher was a shadow in Tumblebrook's folklore, a sentinel over secrets.

Toward the journal's end, one torn page stopped her.

"They're closing in. Martin's gone. I hear them outside. The Watcher is here. If anyone finds this — Beware. They know."

The rest of the page was violently ripped away.

Amelia closed the journal, hands trembling. The storm howled louder, windows rattling like a beast at the door. Lady Grey meowed softly and brushed against Amelia's leg, as if to say, *It's not over.*

Amelia stood, journal pressed to her chest. The scent of damp earth and old paper clung to her sweater. Whatever Annie had uncovered — whatever had cost her everything — was now in Amelia's hands.

And someone — or something — might want it back.

The storm raged outside. But the storm inside Tumblebrook Inn had only just begun.

Chapter 2

The Journal's Whisper

The sun had not yet risen, and Tumblebrook remained cloaked in murky pre-dawn darkness when Clara Henderson's phone buzzed insistently on her nightstand.

Clara groaned, muffled by her pillow, and blinked herself awake. The red digits on the clock glowed: 5:14 a.m. — a time she usually only saw during sleepless nights spent reading. But the name flashing on the screen jolted her to full alert.

Amelia Farnsworth.

Amelia didn't call at odd hours without good reason.

Clara fumbled to answer. "Amelia?"

"Clara, I need you at the inn. Now," Amelia's voice was breathless, tinged with urgency. "It's about Annie."

Clara swung her legs out of bed, her pulse quickening. "Annie? But—"

"Just come," Amelia interrupted. "There's something you need to see."

The line went dead. Clara stared at the screen a moment longer, her thoughts scrambling. Annie Farnsworth. Amelia's great-aunt. A woman lost to Tumblebrook's whispers and ghost stories. And now, after decades of silence, something of hers had resurfaced.

Clara dressed quickly — jeans, a thick cable-knit sweater, and a raincoat that had seen better days. Outside, the wind howled through the narrow streets, rattling shutters and tossing leaves like confetti. The storm had lessened, but a steady drizzle remained.

As she drove through the sleeping town, Clara couldn't shake the feeling of being watched. The closed shopfronts loomed like sentinels. Gossamer Fables stood dark and silent, its windows reflecting the swaying trees. The streets, usually quaint and cozy, now stretched long and empty — as if the town itself held its breath.

The inn glowed like a beacon against the gloom, its lights cutting through the mist. Lady Grey perched on the porch railing, silver fur shining in the lamplight, eyes fixed on the road like she'd been waiting.

"What did you find?" Clara asked, rushing up the steps.

Amelia didn't answer. She opened the door and led Clara into the front parlor, her expression tight. The room was dim, lit only by the soft amber glow of the fire. On the coffee table, surrounded by mugs of tea and scattered papers, lay a weathered leather-bound journal.

Clara's gaze dropped to the faded gold lettering on the cover. Annie Farnsworth.

"You found it in the basement?" she asked, lowering herself onto the couch.

"Behind a false panel," Amelia said, settling into the armchair across from her. "Lady Grey led me right to it."

As if on cue, the cat hopped onto the coffee table and circled the journal once before sitting back, tail twitching.

Clara reached for the journal, its cracked leather cool under her fingertips. As she opened the cover, the scent of aged paper and ink mingled with cinnamon tea and woodsmoke. The handwriting was tight and slanted, the ink slightly smudged, as though written in haste. The first pages listed grocery items, guest notes, and minor repair mentions — the mundane details of innkeeping.

But then the tone shifted. The entries grew chaotic, the handwriting more jagged.

"October 3rd, 1959," Clara read aloud. "Martin said he heard them talking behind the bakery. Something about the sawmill. Said it's best to keep his mouth shut. But I can't ignore what I've seen."

Amelia leaned in, elbows on knees. "Martin Hale. The logger who died."

"Not just died," Clara said, eyes fixed on the page. "Annie didn't think it was an accident. She was convinced someone staged it."

The fire crackled softly, but the room felt colder.

Clara flipped forward. The entries grew frantic, the ink darker.

"October 10th, 1959. Strange lights down by the river again. Martin said he'd show me where he found the tracks. But he never came. Sheriff said it was a logging accident, but Martin knew the woods. No way he'd walk beneath a falling tree."

Amelia's jaw clenched. "And no way the sheriff would challenge the Harringtons' version of events."

Clara nodded. She turned to a torn entry. The jagged edges suggested haste. A few scrawled words remained:

"Saw him last night. Watching. Eyes like shadows. Said I knew too much. Must hide the rest — before they find it."

Clara's throat tightened. "She was being watched."

"By who?" Amelia murmured, her hand resting protectively over the journal.

Before Clara could respond, Lady Grey let out a plaintive yowl and bounded to the far side of the room. She stopped at the base of the fireplace, tail puffed, batting at the stonework.

Amelia and Clara exchanged a glance.

"What is it, girl?" Amelia asked, rising.

Lady Grey meowed again, more insistent now.

Clara joined her. The cat's pupils were wide. Amelia pressed against the stone, testing for movement. One block shifted. Behind it, a small recess.

Inside, a rusted tin box.

Amelia lifted it out, her pulse racing. She pried it open — inside, a bundle of letters tied with frayed twine. The names on the envelopes caught Clara's breath.

"Martin Hale," she whispered. "Nathaniel Wescott. Edgar Harrington."

Amelia's eyes sharpened. "The key players in Martin's death."

Clara untied the bundle and opened the first letter. The ink was smudged but legible:

"Annie, They know what we talked about. If I disappear, look to the lake. The truth is there. But be careful. They're watching. – M"

Clara's hands trembled. "Martin was trying to warn her."

"And now he's warning us," Amelia said, voice low but fierce.

They stared down at the letters, pieces of a puzzle buried for over sixty years. Lady Grey purred low, gaze still fixed on the tin box as if expecting more secrets to crawl out.

"If Annie was right," Clara whispered, "then everything we thought about Martin's death was a lie."

"And the truth," Amelia said, lifting the box, "is finally coming to light."

A gust of wind howled through the chimney, hollow and mournful. Outside, the rain poured again, pounding the windows like a warning.

Something had been set in motion. There would be no stopping it now.

Chapter 3

Shadows in the Hall

The morning after the storm dawned clear and cold, the air sharp with the scent of wet leaves and ozone. Sunlight glinted off puddles that dotted the cobblestone drive, casting tiny prisms of light — a deceptively cheerful contrast to the unease threading through Amelia Farnsworth's veins.

Inside the Tumblebrook Inn, the breakfast room hummed with the low murmur of guests exchanging pleasantries over steaming cups of coffee and warm cinnamon scones. It was a typical morning — on the surface. But beneath the polite chatter pulsed a darker undercurrent.

Amelia moved through the room with a pot of fresh coffee, her smile warm, but her gaze sharper than usual. Her mind remained trapped in the basement, turning over every word of Annie's journal like a stone in her palm. Murder. Beware. Those words echoed in her thoughts, casting shadows across the ordinary bustle of the morning service.

"Did you hear that wind last night?" one guest asked, leaning over his cup of coffee. "Sounded like a banshee."

"I swore I saw someone by the lake," said another, eyes wide. "Just a shadow — but it was there."

"Probably just the old place settling," someone else offered with a forced chuckle. "Or maybe the inn's haunted."

Haunted. The word lodged in Amelia's chest like a thorn. Haunted by what? By whom?

Lady Grey sauntered in, her amber eyes scanning the room with the scrutiny of a seasoned detective. Her movements were precise, deliberate, as though assessing each guest in turn. She brushed against Amelia's leg before leaping to the windowsill, ears perked, gaze narrowed.

The front door banged open. A gust of cold wind swept through the room, sending a chill up Amelia's spine. She turned sharply, heart hammering — only to see Mr. Godwin, the antique dealer from Duluth, stomping snow from his boots. His ruddy face broke into a grin.

"Mornin', Ms. Farnsworth!"

Amelia forced a smile, her grip tightening on the coffee pot. "Morning, Mr. Godwin. Coffee?"

"Please and thank you," he said, still shivering. "Nasty storm last night."

"Yes," Amelia murmured, pouring the coffee while scanning the room. The inn was full — a tour group from St. Paul, locals escaping power outages, and a few out-of-towners with oddly vague stories. Every conversation felt laced with subtext. Every smile seemed just a little too fixed.

"And how are you this fine morning?" Mr. Godwin asked, oblivious to the tension in her shoulders.

"Oh, you know," Amelia said with a hollow laugh. "Just another day at the inn."

But it wasn't just another day. The inn wasn't just an inn anymore. It was a stage, and the players were already in motion.

Later that morning, with the breakfast crowd dispersed and Lady Grey curled in a sunbeam by the stairs, Amelia and Clara huddled in the inn's private lounge. The small room, usually a retreat for quiet guests, now served as their war room.

Annie's journal lay open on the table, its brittle pages like an open wound. Beside it sat the tin box, its contents — letters, clippings, and the strange trinket they'd found — arranged like a puzzle waiting to be solved.

"Look here," Clara said, brow furrowed as she traced a line of Annie's spidery script. "October 7th, 1959. 'Met R.H. at the silver birch clearing. Told me to stop asking questions. Said Martin's death was an accident, but his eyes said something else. He knows. They all know.'"

"R.H.," Amelia murmured, fingers drumming on the table. "Russell Harrington."

"Or his father," Clara said grimly. "Either way, it's the Harringtons. The same family that owns half the town."

Amelia leaned back, eyes fixed on the ceiling. "So Annie was poking around, asking questions about Martin's death, and the Harringtons wanted her to stop."

"They threatened her," Clara said, tapping the page. "And they weren't the only ones."

"Meaning?"

Clara flipped forward to a later entry, dated two weeks later. "'Saw him again by the lake. Eyes like shadows. Said they were watching me. Said they'd take everything from me if I didn't stop. Don't know who to trust anymore.'"

Amelia's stomach churned. "The Watcher."

"Exactly," Clara said. "If he was watching Annie, who's to say he's not watching us?"

Lady Grey lifted her head, ears twitching. She stretched and padded toward the far side of the room. Clara watched, frowning as the cat grew more insistent. Lady Grey batted at the baseboard, claws scraping wood.

Amelia and Clara exchanged a glance.

"She's found something," Clara whispered.

They knelt beside the cat. Lady Grey meowed sharply, eyes locked on a spot beneath the wainscoting. Amelia pressed her hands against the wood, fingers searching. There — a slight give.

With a soft creak, a panel slid open. Inside: a small, tarnished pendant. Shaped like an oak tree, its branches twisted into a circular pattern. At its center: a polished, deep blue stone.

"This symbol," Clara whispered, turning it over. "It's the Harrington crest."

Amelia's blood ran cold. "So Annie was right. They were watching her."

Clara nodded, eyes dark. "And they might still be watching us."

A gust of wind rattled the windows. In the firelight, the pendant's stone gleamed like an unblinking eye. Lady Grey sat back, tail curled, gaze fixed on the hallway.

"They never stopped watching," Amelia murmured, clutching the pendant. "They've been watching all along."

Chapter 4

Rumors That Linger

The bell above the door to Gossamer Fables jingled softly as Clara Henderson stepped inside, the scent of old pages, beeswax, and rain-dampened wool greeting her like an embrace. Outside, the storm had left Tumblebrook's sidewalks slick and shining, and the hushed interior of the bookshop felt like a sanctuary — a pocket of stillness in a town where the past was rising like mist from the lake.

"Morning, Clara," called Mr. Lark, the proprietor, from behind the counter. His cardigan was buttoned crookedly, and his hair stood up in unkempt tufts, as though he hadn't slept. He was arranging a display of local folklore books on the nearby table. "You're in early."

Clara gave him a small smile as she peeled off her coat and shook the damp from her scarf. "It's one of those mornings."

Mr. Lark nodded knowingly, his gaze lingering a beat too long. "Been hearing a lot of strange things lately," he murmured, lowering his voice. "People talking about ghosts. Shadows in the woods."

Clara's stomach tightened. "You don't say."

"Old stories don't always stay buried," he said, his eyes shadowed. "Be careful what you dig up."

Before Clara could respond, he turned away, his shoulders stiff beneath the worn wool. Clara moved deeper into the shop, her boots echoing softly against the hardwood. The shelves loomed around her like silent sentinels, spines gleaming with faded gold.

She wandered to the back, passing sections she could navigate blindfolded. The trinket Amelia had found pulsed in her mind — its twisted oak tree design, the dark stone glinting like an unblinking eye. The inn had always held secrets, but now it seemed the entire town was complicit in keeping them.

Clara pulled three volumes from the local history section: *Timber and Town: The Early Days of Tumblebrook, Emblems of the North Shore,* and *The Harrington Legacy.* She hesitated over the last one, fingers brushing the gilded spine. The Harringtons. Their reach stretched through Tumblebrook's history like roots beneath the ground — unseen but unyielding.

She carried the books to a back table, where a reading lamp cast a warm glow. Outside, rain fell in a steady drizzle, distorting the glass view into the alley. The streetlamp's light glimmered faintly in the fog.

Clara settled in, quickly absorbed. Each page was a window into a Tumblebrook few dared to discuss — lumber barons, secret land deals, and a shadowy group referred to only as "The Order."

Her pulse quickened as she flipped to a grainy black-and-white photograph. A group of men in dark suits stood before the old Tumblebrook Sawmill. Among them were the town's most influential — a young Russell Harrington, his father, and Edgar Hale. Clara's eyes caught the pins they wore — identical to the trinket Amelia had found, each marked with the oak tree emblem and a dark stone at its center.

Emblem of the Pledged, the caption read.

Pledged to what? Clara wondered, heart pounding. The text was vague, referencing a brotherhood forged in secrecy to "preserve Tumblebrook's interests." But what interests? And what had they been willing to do to protect them?

"You researching the old families?"

The voice came from behind. Clara started, nearly knocking over her coffee. A man stood a few feet away. Tall, lean, with silver-streaked hair and a raincoat still damp from the storm. His face was unfamiliar, but his eyes were dark, sharp — focused on the book.

"I'm sorry," Clara said, closing the book halfway. "Do I know you?"

"No," he said with a thin smile. "Just noticed you were digging into some... obscure topics."

Clara forced a chuckle. "I work here part-time. Just brushing up on the town's history."

"The Order isn't just history," he said softly. "It's a legacy. Some stories are better left alone."

Clara's fingers tightened on the book. "Are you a historian?"

"Something like that," he said, eyes gleaming. "Just be careful. Some stories aren't meant to be told."

Before she could reply, Mr. Lark called from the counter. "Clara! The new inventory list — can you grab it?"

Clara stood, her knees stiff. "Sure."

When she returned a moment later, the man was gone. Only a single, wet footprint remained on the wooden floor — a dark smear pointing toward the door.

Back at the inn, Amelia sorted the morning's mail. Bills. A flyer for bulk tea. A postcard from a spring guest. And one envelope with no return address.

She turned it over slowly. The handwriting was narrow, slanted — unfamiliar. Lady Grey leapt onto the counter, her amber eyes fixed on the envelope, ears twitching.

Amelia tore it open, her heart hammering. Inside: a single piece of paper, the ink smudged.

Some questions should remain unanswered. Let sleeping dogs lie.

Lady Grey growled low, her fur bristling. Amelia dropped the letter as though it burned. The words blurred, each one a warning.

Lady Grey leapt to the floor and padded to the basement door, her tail twitching urgently.

"Not now," Amelia whispered, but the cat meowed again, louder this time, eyes wide.

Downstairs, the basement was colder than usual. The scent of damp earth and old wood clung to everything. Lady Grey moved straight to the far corner, nose pressed to a stack of old crates.

Amelia pushed them aside, her pulse thudding. The floorboards creaked. One lifted just enough to slip her fingers beneath.

Wrapped in a mildewed rag was another notebook. Annie's handwriting danced across the first page, dark and urgent:

They're watching. Eyes everywhere.

Amelia shivered, the notebook heavy in her hand.

An hour later, Clara arrived, cheeks flushed, hair damp. "Amelia, we need to talk."

They sat in the study, the notebook open between them, Lady Grey pacing restlessly.

"I think The Order is real," Clara said, voice trembling. "I think they're still here."

Amelia slid the anonymous letter across the table. "I think they know we're looking."

Clara read the note, her eyes widening. Outside, a shadow flickered past the window. Lady Grey stopped pacing, gaze fixed on the darkened hallway beyond.

Silence stretched — thick as the fog rolling off the lake. A log cracked in the fireplace, and both women jumped.

"We're being watched," Clara whispered.

Amelia nodded, jaw clenched. "And they're not going to let us keep digging without a fight."

Chapter 5

The Quiet Before the Storm

The morning mist rolled off the lake like a slow breath, blanketing Tumblebrook in a silvery hush. The storm had passed, leaving behind damp earth, fallen leaves, and a rare lull in the town's usual rustling rhythms. But for Amelia Farnsworth, the quiet only sharpened her unease. It was too still — as if the town itself were holding its breath.

She stood on the porch of the Tumblebrook Inn, a steaming mug of Earl Grey in her hands, watching the sun rise over the water. Lady Grey sat beside her, tail wrapped neatly around her paws, gaze fixed not on the view but on something unseen across the road — beyond the trees. Her amber eyes narrowed, flicking once toward a crooked oak before locking into a steady, unblinking stare.

Amelia followed the cat's gaze. Nothing moved. No wind stirred the branches. But a sliver of discomfort tightened between her shoulders. She recognized that look in Lady Grey's eyes. The cat sensed something — or someone. The unease coiled in Amelia's chest like a snake. She took another sip of tea, the steam curling up to mingle with the mist, and tried to shake the feeling clinging to her like cobwebs.

Behind her, Clara's footsteps creaked across the porch. "I've been thinking," Clara said, handing her a folded piece of paper. "Last night I reviewed Annie's notes again. The way she circled certain names, the phrases she repeated — 'tangled loyalties,' 'wronged hearts.' I think there's more to this than land and lumber."

Amelia nodded, scanning the notes. "Affairs?"

"Maybe. Family betrayals. Old romances turned sour. Someone powerful with something to lose." Clara sighed, pulling her cardigan tighter. "I think someone got desperate. Desperate enough to kill."

That brought Amelia to her next plan.

She set down her tea and reached for her coat. "I'm going to visit Millie."

* * *

Millie Jefferson's cottage sat just past the church on Hemlock Lane, a sun-faded structure with flower boxes still brimming with marigolds and mums despite the season. Inside, warmth wrapped around Amelia like a shawl — clove, cinnamon, and the tang of lemon oil. Millie, bundled in a raspberry-colored wrap, answered the door with a cheerful, "You come bearing baked goods?"

Amelia held up a paper bag. "Still warm."

They settled at the kitchen table, cinnamon buns between them, and Lady Grey leapt onto the windowsill. Sunlight filtered through sheer curtains, turning dust motes into gold. The air held a trace of honey and lavender — the kind of scent that clings to old houses and older memories.

After a few sips of coffee and some catching up, Amelia leaned forward.

"I need to ask about something that happened years ago. About Martin Hale."

Millie's smile faltered. "I was a girl, but I remember the whispers."

"What kind of whispers?"

Millie stared into her cup. "People said Martin wasn't just another logger. He was sweet on someone he shouldn't have been."

"Someone married?"

Millie hesitated. "Engaged. To a Harrington, if the talk was true. But her name was never spoken aloud. Folks were careful. Especially with the Harringtons."

"Was Annie involved?"

"Your great-aunt? No. Though I think she knew more than she ever said. She and Martin were... friendly. But not like that."

Millie rose and crossed the room, retrieving a yellowed envelope from a drawer. "I found this in my mother's sewing box years ago. Don't ask how it got there."

Inside was a photo — Martin, smiling beside a woman whose face had been scratched out. On the back, in faded ink: *Birch Hollow, July 1959.*

"Birch Hollow," Amelia whispered. "That's near the woods Annie marked."

Millie nodded. "Strange things started happening after that summer. People left town quietly. Others kept their mouths shut. But we all felt it — the silence that settled in like fog. A kind of shared forgetting."

Amelia tucked the photo away and reached for Millie's hand. "Thank you. This helps more than you know."

Millie squeezed gently. "Just be careful, dear. Some stories are buried for a reason. And some people will do anything to keep them that way."

* * *

Later, back at the inn, Clara met Amelia in the lounge, where a dozen maps, notes, and journal pages were strewn across the table. The room smelled of wax and woodsmoke; the fireplace crackled faintly. Lady Grey leapt onto the armchair, scattering a pile of papers.

"Lady!" Amelia began — then paused.

Beneath the pages was a folded sheet of brittle paper, wedged deep in the spine of Annie's journal. Amelia tugged it free.

It was a hand-drawn map, the black ink faded to gray. Paths. Tree names. A stream. And an X marked just beyond the silver birch grove.

"Clara," she whispered. "She hid this."

Clara leaned in. "That spot... it's just north of the lake trail."

"I know it," Amelia said. "Near the clearing where the children used to build forts. I played there as a girl."

"Do you think the X marks where Martin was found?"

"Or where Annie found something she wasn't supposed to."

They moved quickly — boots, thermoses, flashlights, notebooks. They'd leave at dawn. Less chance of being followed. Or watched. Clara suggested a side trail, one less traveled. Amelia packed a compass, first aid kit, and a spare pair of gloves. Lady Grey paced between them, chirping as if offering her own advice.

But as Amelia passed the mantel, her gaze fell on the small wooden box where she kept the trinket.

It was open.

Empty.

Her stomach dropped. "Clara?"

Clara turned, instantly alert.

"It's gone."

Clara's eyes widened. "The brooch?"

Amelia nodded. "Someone's been inside."

Lady Grey sat motionless at the foot of the stairs, her ears flat, tail thumping once. She stared into the dark hallway.

Someone had been inside.

And they'd taken the trinket.

The fire popped in the hearth. Outside, the wind began to rise again, brushing leaves against the shutters like restless fingers. Whatever had been dormant was stirring. A gust rattled the windowpanes, and Amelia stepped closer to the glass.

Nothing but shadows.

They would go to the woods at dawn.

But tonight, they would sleep with the doors bolted and their eyes open.

Chapter 6

Into the Woods

The first pale light of dawn slipped over the horizon like a whisper, brushing the treetops in gold and ash. The forest on the edge of Tumblebrook held a stillness that felt ancient, as though it had been waiting for someone to step into its heart. The rustle of leaves sounded almost ceremonial, as if the woods were preparing to witness something long overdue. Above, a hawk circled lazily, casting a fleeting shadow across the path ahead.

Clara Henderson adjusted the straps of her backpack and glanced toward Amelia, who stood nearby tightening her bootlaces. Lady Grey circled their feet, her tail flicking with purposeful energy. The air smelled of damp moss, crisp leaves, and a faint trace of woodsmoke drifting from distant chimneys. Insects buzzed lazily in the cool air, and a woodpecker drummed somewhere high in the canopy. In the distance, the lake glimmered faintly through a break in the trees, its still waters mirroring the sleepy sky.

"You sure about this path?" Amelia asked quietly, unfolding Annie's map. Her voice was low, unwilling to disturb the hush.

Clara nodded. "This trail cuts northeast, curves around Birch

Hollow, then heads into the old-growth near the lake. Annie marked it clearly."

Amelia gave a short nod. "Then let's go—before someone decides to follow."

They set off, boots crunching softly on fallen leaves. The trees closed in around them, tall and whispering. Mist wove through the trunks like breath. Birds stirred, their calls faint and cautious. Lady Grey darted ahead, her grey coat nearly blending with the underbrush. She paused often to glance back, checking their pace.

The farther they walked, the deeper the silence seemed to grow. Clara studied the path carefully, noting subtle breaks in branches and the occasional scuff in the leaf litter—signs that someone had passed not long ago. Her instincts sharpened. The forest felt transformed— not just a place of nature, but a keeper of secrets.

They moved through groves of sugar maple and ash, past crumbling stone markers swallowed by moss. At one point, a half-collapsed fence ran beside the trail, its purpose long forgotten.

Clara knelt, touching the rusted wire. "This was a boundary once. A family property line, maybe. Someone wanted to keep this part of the forest contained."

"Or keep people out," Amelia murmured.

A fox darted across the trail ahead—a flash of red in the green. They paused, exchanged glances, and pressed on. Sunlight filtered through the canopy in shifting ribbons, painting the path in gold and green.

An hour passed in relative quiet until they reached a fork not shown on any town-maintained maps. Clara held up the journal.

"According to Annie's sketch, we take the left fork. The right goes to the fishing docks."

Amelia hesitated. "You think anyone uses this path?"

"Maybe. But Annie called it the Forgotten Spine. She was certain no one went this way anymore."

They pressed on. The trail narrowed, tree roots breaking through the ground like gnarled veins. A crow cawed overhead, startling Clara.

"We're fine," she muttered, though her grip tightened on the journal.

Thirty minutes later, Clara spotted something ahead—a weather-worn sign barely visible through the brush. It leaned on a broken post, its paint nearly gone. One word remained: "Hollow."

"We're close," she whispered.

Lady Grey suddenly stopped and sat in the center of the trail.

"What is it?" Amelia asked.

Clara followed the cat's gaze—and saw it too. A small structure nestled in the dense trees. Its wood darkened with age, moss clinging to the roof. A crooked door hung ajar.

"The cabin," Clara breathed.

They approached cautiously. Every crunch of leaf and groan of wood beneath their boots felt too loud. A faded path, long overtaken by brambles, led to the porch. Faded boot prints marked the edge. Vines climbed the siding, and the remnants of a porch swing creaked faintly.

Inside, the air was stale and thick with dust. A sliver of light cut through a crack in the wall, illuminating floating motes. The room was sparse—a rusted bedframe, a collapsed chair, and a cast-iron stove. A faded curtain still clung to one window. Beneath it, an old trunk lay under the sill, its latch rusted shut.

Lady Grey leapt to the broken chair, sniffed, then to the hearth. She pawed at a loose panel beneath the stones.

"Here," Clara said, rushing over.

They pried the panel loose with a pocketknife. Beneath it lay a faded oilcloth bundle. Clara carefully unwrapped it.

Inside were yellowed newspaper clippings, a torn journal page, and black-and-white photographs. One showed Martin Hale beside a woman whose face had been gouged out—just like the photo Millie had shown them. Another clipping read: *LOGGER TRAGEDY AT BIRCH HOLLOW*.

There was also a small brass key tied with twine. Old and ornate, its head bore an emblem—an oak tree with curling branches. The same emblem from the missing brooch.

Amelia scanned the clippings. "These were hidden deliberately."

"Someone didn't want the town remembering this," Clara said. "Someone went to great lengths to keep this place hidden."

Then a floorboard creaked—just outside.

Clara froze. Amelia went still.

Lady Grey darted beneath the stove.

Footsteps. Slow. Deliberate. Getting closer.

Clara held her breath. Amelia motioned for silence, pointing toward the cabin's back.

There was a crawl space beneath the floorboards—half-rotted but just large enough. They scrambled to lift a board as quietly as possible and slid into the narrow space, pulling the panel shut.

Clara lay flat on the damp earth, heart pounding. Amelia clutched the documents tightly. Lady Grey crouched between them, ears twitching.

The door creaked open.

Footsteps entered. A figure moved across the floor.

Through the cracks, Clara glimpsed boots—sturdy and expensive. Not a hunter. Not a hiker.

The intruder paused at the hearth. The chair creaked. The footsteps shifted.

A heavy sigh.

Then the boots turned.

Steps toward the door.

Clara didn't breathe until the sound faded completely.

Amelia waited five long minutes.

Then whispered, "We need to go."

But, footsteps just outside the cabin again. Their bodies frozen, barely able to breathe. They were back.

"I think we've been found," Amelia whispered."

Chapter 7

Watchful Eyes

The stillness inside the crawl space was suffocating.

Amelia Farnsworth barely breathed. Damp earth pressed against her cheek, and every heartbeat seemed too loud. Dust floated in the dim beams of light that peeked through gaps in the floorboards above. Next to her, Clara remained motionless, her fingers clenched tightly around the bundle of hidden documents. Lady Grey huddled between them, unusually subdued, as if she, too, sensed the gravity of the moment. Even the air felt heavier—thick with tension, mold, and old wood.

Above them, footsteps creaked—two sets now.

Amelia held her breath and leaned toward the slat above her face, careful not to shift it. Her green eyes narrowed as she caught glimpses of the two figures moving above.

The first was a man—tall, broad-shouldered, wearing an oilskin coat that shimmered faintly with moisture. The second figure was slimmer, cloaked in a gray jacket, the hood drawn up. From this angle, Amelia couldn't see their faces, but their body language set her nerves on edge.

"We shouldn't be here," the hooded figure whispered, their voice tight.

"Too late for that," the man snapped. "She's already found something. I told you it was only a matter of time."

Amelia squinted, trying to place the voice.

"If it leaks—the affair, the ledgers, the fire—it won't just be scandal. It'll burn the whole town."

The hooded figure stepped closer to the hearth—right above Lady Grey, who didn't flinch.

"I warned you," they said. "Hiding it doesn't erase it."

The man grunted. "I told you to bury it. Let sleeping dogs lie."

A chair scraped. "We need to go. We're exposed here."

The footsteps retreated—slow at first, then faster—vanishing into the forest.

Amelia exhaled slowly. Her heart pounded in her ears. A sharp stone dug into her ribs, but she barely noticed.

Several minutes passed before she whispered, "They're gone."

Clara lifted the loose board an inch and peeked out. When it was clear, they emerged, brushing off dirt and stretching sore limbs. Lady Grey leapt out daintily, shaking dust from her coat.

Amelia moved to the doorway. Nothing but quiet. The eerie stillness following the figures' departure only heightened the tension. A crow cawed somewhere. A breeze stirred the leaves. But the forest felt frozen.

"We should head back," Clara said, tucking the bundle deeper into her bag.

"At nightfall," Amelia agreed. "Too risky in daylight."

They waited in the shadows two more hours, sharing a flask of water and the silence that follows shared danger. As the light waned, the woods grew colder. They whispered theories and names—Harrington, Pike—piecing together implications. Clara jotted notes by lantern light, sketching the cabin's location and quoting key phrases.

Amelia paced quietly, eyes scanning the trees. Every branch snap set them on edge. When darkness finally fell, they slipped from the cabin and crept back to town, hugging deer trails and sticking to the trees. The trip took twice as long, and not a word passed between them.

* * *

The inn loomed ahead, its porch casting long shadows over the gravel drive. Lanterns flickered on one by one down Main Street, amber halos in the growing dark.

Inside, Amelia's legs ached, but adrenaline kept her sharp. Every creak made her spine straighten.

Clara eased open the back door. "No signs of forced entry," she whispered.

Lady Grey darted inside, alert and sniffing corners. Her ears twitched with every creak. Her pupils, wide.

Amelia stepped into the kitchen. The scent of cinnamon and lemon balm lingered, a ghost of normalcy. For a heartbeat, she longed to pretend nothing had changed. But the lantern shadows stretched longer than they should have.

Clara dropped her bag on the table. "We have to call someone. The police maybe."

Amelia hesitated. "And say what? That we followed a map to a rotting cabin and overheard two people discussing a decades-old cover-up?"

Clara opened her mouth, then shut it. "You're right. They'd laugh us out."

Amelia moved toward the fireplace, hands on her hips. Lady Grey jumped onto the mantel and nudged the clock. Then she reached behind a framed photo—Amelia's favorite of Annie—and tapped something.

Her paw snagged a folded slip of paper.

"Another journal page," Clara breathed.

Amelia unfolded it. Annie's handwriting flowed across the aged paper:

I trusted him. I believed he would protect me. But betrayal wears a familiar face. If anything happens to me, the truth lies not in the woods —but beneath our feet.

They stared at the final line.

Clara's voice dropped to a whisper. "You don't think she meant the inn?"

Amelia's spine tingled. "We're standing on it, aren't we?"

The kitchen light flickered.

Then again.

Then everything went dark.

Lady Grey meowed, low and steady—a warning.

Outside, wind howled. Shutters rattled. A branch scraped across the roof. Darkness swallowed the inn.

Amelia fumbled for a lantern by the pantry. The wick caught, casting a fragile pool of light. Clara grabbed the flashlight from the cellar steps. Still working.

"Storm?" Clara asked.

Amelia shook her head. "Feels intentional."

Lady Grey padded from the room. She paused near the parlor and meowed again.

Amelia followed with the lantern. The windows were pitch-black. She checked the locks—secure. Then the basement door.

Also locked.

"What did Annie mean?" Clara asked. "What's beneath our feet?"

Amelia's gaze drifted to the cellar. "There's a bricked-over alcove behind the wine shelves. Annie used to call it the root cellar, but she never kept anything there."

They stood in flickering light, realization dawning.

A draft blew from under the basement door.

Lady Grey scratched once at the parlor floor, then sat. Her golden eyes locked on the darkness.

Tomorrow, they would unearth secrets.

Tonight, they would stand guard over the truth.

Chapter 8

The Light Within

The darkness had teeth.

Clara Henderson sat at the edge of her bed, flashlight in one hand, the other gripping the edge of a blanket wrapped tightly around her shoulders. The walls of Tumblebrook Inn creaked with wind and age, and every sound—every distant rustle, groan of floorboards, or shifting of old pipes—felt sharpened in the absence of light. Somewhere downstairs, Amelia moved with careful purpose, checking each lock for the third time. Lady Grey's occasional meow was the only reminder that the world beyond hadn't gone entirely mad.

The power outage had lasted longer than expected.

Too long.

And though Clara was the rational one—the one who clung to logic and data like life rafts in a sea of sentiment—even she felt the edges of unease creeping closer. This wasn't a simple blackout. This was targeted. It had weight and purpose—like a curtain being drawn before a play's climax. In all her years working in Tumblebrook, nothing had ever felt this coordinated.

A gust of wind rattled her window. She jumped.

Taking a steadying breath, she flipped through Annie's journal again, its fragile pages worn from repeated handling. She stopped on one she'd marked earlier:

When the shadows press in and trust wears thin, remember this: light doesn't come from the lantern. It burns within.

She read the line again.

It wasn't the poetry that struck her, nor the metaphor.

It was the challenge.

Clara pushed the blanket away and stood, gripping her flashlight like a torch. The cold air prickled her skin, but her mind buzzed with clarity. Her instincts, usually governed by method and reason, now danced on the edge of something more visceral: intuition.

She descended the stairs slowly, flashlight casting long shadows along the hallway. A floorboard creaked behind her. She whirled, but nothing was there.

Downstairs, Amelia sat in the parlor by the fireplace, a notebook in her lap and firelight flickering across her features. She glanced up.

"Couldn't sleep?" she asked.

Clara shook her head. "Can you?"

Amelia gave a dry smile. "Didn't even try."

Lady Grey perched on the arm of the settee, tail wrapped around her feet, staring into the fire like a philosopher.

Clara settled into the armchair opposite. "I keep going over what they said at the cabin."

"The fire, the ledgers, the affair," Amelia said, nodding. "All connected somehow."

Clara leaned forward. "And Annie's words... *the truth lies beneath.* I don't think she was just being poetic. I think there's more hidden in this house than we realized."

"You think it's connected to the bricked alcove in the cellar?"

Clara nodded. "Maybe evidence. Maybe a record. Maybe someone—some family—used the inn as a front or a meeting place."

Amelia reached into a box beside her and pulled out a stack of photographs—old black-and-whites from the inn's early days. "I found these earlier. Recognize anyone?"

Clara shuffled through them, pausing on one: a young couple standing beneath the garden arbor, smiling but stiff. The man wore a dark suit, the woman a floral dress. The date on the back read *1959*.

She frowned. "He looks like Martin Hale."

"I thought so too," Amelia said. "And the woman—does she look familiar?"

Clara stared. "She looks like Eleanor Harrington."

Amelia leaned forward. "What if the affair wasn't just rumor? What if it was real—and she chose him?"

"And paid the price," Clara whispered.

They sat in silence for a moment, the fire crackling softly. Wind howled outside, and the flames trembled.

Then Lady Grey stood, stretched, and padded toward the cellar door.

"Third time tonight," Amelia muttered. "She wants us to see something."

Clara stood. "Then let's go."

The cellar was colder than usual. Clara's breath misted in front of her flashlight beam. The walls were lined with bottles of wine, dusty preserves, and jars of lavender Amelia insisted on keeping for stress relief. But their destination was the far corner—where a section of brickwork didn't match the rest.

Clara knelt and ran her fingers along the mortar. It crumbled under pressure. Her flashlight danced over faint scratches at the base —marks that might once have been initials or symbols.

Amelia handed her a chisel and mallet from the utility cabinet. "Let's hope this isn't just structural reinforcement."

Clara tapped carefully at the edges, loosening bricks one by one. Dust filled the air. Behind the final layer was a hollow.

Inside lay a tarnished metal box, locked with an old latch.

Amelia exhaled. "There it is."

They carried it upstairs and set it on the kitchen table. Clara wiped the surface and found a tiny emblem etched into the lid—an oak tree with curling roots.

"The same emblem from the brooch," Amelia said. "And the map."

Clara picked the lock with a hairpin and patience. It popped open with a soft click.

Inside were folded papers, faded photographs, and a black leather-bound book. The scent of must and time rose up like a whisper from the past.

Clara opened the book first. It was a guest ledger.

But the names weren't just guests—they were initials, often accompanied by payment amounts, meeting dates, and—oddest of all —descriptions of goods: *barrel, ledger, map.*

"It's a record," she whispered. "Not of guests... but of transactions. Hidden ones."

The lights snapped on. They blinked at the sudden brightness. The fixtures hummed faintly, casting harsh light over the old papers.

Then the phone rang.

Chapter 9

The Missing Guest

Amelia Farnsworth stood in the kitchen of the Tumblebrook Inn, the telephone receiver still warm in her hand. The world around her buzzed with a low, electric dread — the lights had returned, yes, but the tension hadn't lifted. If anything, it had deepened. A missing guest. A false name. A quiet man with questions in his eyes and secrets under his coat. Carlton Maddox — or whoever he truly was — had vanished, and with his disappearance, the investigation had taken a dangerous turn.

She hung up the phone slowly and turned to Clara, who stood nearby with a tea towel clenched tightly in her hand. "He wasn't who he said he was," Amelia said.

Clara's brows knit together. "What do you mean?"

"The officer said the name doesn't match any license or ID on record. They think it was fabricated. They're trying to find out more, but... they don't sound hopeful."

Clara crossed her arms and leaned back against the counter. "And he was in Room Five."

Amelia nodded grimly. "If he knew what we were chasing — and came here for it — we need to find out what he left behind."

Together, they climbed the stairs to the second floor. The inn was quiet, most guests still asleep, oblivious to the brewing storm. Each footstep on the old wood felt louder than usual, as though the house itself was holding its breath. Room Five sat at the end of the hall, its door slightly ajar, as if it had been waiting for them. Each step echoed with the weight of what they feared they might find — or not find.

Amelia pushed it open. The room was neat, untouched since that morning's housekeeping. The bed had been made, the curtains drawn. It looked as though no one had ever stayed there. But Amelia knew better.

They began their search in silence, falling into a rhythm honed by days of quiet investigation.

Amelia moved to the nightstand, pulling out the drawer. Nothing. A pen, a complimentary notepad, and a Gideon's Bible. She lifted the mattress. Nothing. No suitcase in the closet. No toiletries in the bathroom. Everything had been wiped clean, as if someone had erased every trace of a man who clearly had something to hide.

"He cleaned up," she said.

Clara knelt by the heater vent. "Maybe too well."

She unscrewed the vent cover and reached inside. A small envelope, brittle and yellowed, had been taped to the inside of the duct. Clara held it up with a tremble of excitement.

Amelia took it gently and opened it. Inside were three items: a newspaper clipping from 1959, a hand-drawn map of the northern woods near Birch Hollow, and a photograph. The clipping was about Martin Hale, the logger found dead near the riverbank. The official cause had been ruled an accident — blunt force trauma from a fall.

But someone had underlined a phrase in red pen: "...no signs of a struggle."

The map was more detailed than Annie's. It showed trails, cabin sites, and an area labeled: "TR #3 – Coffer Entrance."

"What's a coffer entrance?" Clara asked.

Amelia stared at the drawing. "I think it's an old logging term.

Coffer dams were used to control river flow during timber transport. Maybe this was a site where logs were stored or diverted."

Clara leaned closer. "And maybe where someone hid something."

The photograph chilled her most. It was black and white, slightly faded, but unmistakable: four men in front of a supply shed. One was Martin Hale. Another looked eerily like Edgar Harrington — patriarch of the noble Harrington family.

She turned the photo over. Scrawled in pencil: "July 2, 1959 – Before the end."

Amelia sat down on the edge of the bed. "He was investigating the same thing. The logging accident. The cover-up. And he knew it had to do with the Harringtons."

Clara looked toward the window. "He probably thought we were part of it. Until he realized we were just stumbling toward it too."

Amelia turned the map over. More handwriting.

Check the archive. 3rd floor. Ledger.

"Archive?" Clara asked.

"There's a third floor in the historical society," Amelia said slowly. "It's closed to the public. Only used for preservation and records they don't want touched."

"And it mentions a ledger — same word from Annie's journal, from the box in the cellar."

Amelia felt a throb behind her eyes. The pieces were coming together — too fast, too sharp. Carlton Maddox hadn't come to the inn to rest. He'd come hunting. Just like Annie.

Clara sat beside her. "And now he's gone."

They stared at the evidence in her lap. The room had been scrubbed clean, but secrets had soaked into the walls. The temperature seemed to drop the longer they sat, as though the shadows pressed a little closer, whispering that they were on borrowed time.

A knock on the door startled them both.

It was Millie Jefferson, bundled in a thick shawl and gripping a folded newspaper. "I thought you should see this."

She handed the front page to Amelia. A photo of a twisted sedan, windshield shattered and side door ripped open, stared back at them. The caption read: "Abandoned Car Found at Edge of Pines — Belongs to Tumblebrook Inn Guest."

Clara sucked in a breath. "That's him."

Amelia scanned the article. Police were treating it as suspicious. The car was discovered just off the old mill road, near the entrance to the state forest. No blood. No signs of struggle. Just a car left behind, the door swung wide like a scream.

"He didn't leave," Amelia whispered.

"He was taken," Clara said.

Chapter 10

Upper Hand

Clara Henderson tapped her fingers against the folder in her lap, the rhythm steady but anxious. The morning sun filtered through the lace curtains of the Tumblebrook Inn's parlor, illuminating dust motes that danced slowly in the golden light. Amelia sat across from her, sipping tea with a stillness that belied the storm both of them carried inside. Outside, the air was crisp with the scent of late-autumn pine and the promise of frost, but inside, the inn felt like a pressure cooker about to hiss.

"We can't ignore this anymore," Clara said finally, her voice low but firm, sharpened by sleeplessness and resolve. Her red-rimmed eyes flicked over the file again, as if hoping some overlooked clue would leap off the page. Each handwritten note, circled date, and blurry photo spoke of things long buried—things that didn't want to stay that way.

Amelia glanced up. "You're thinking about the police."

"I am. We have maps, notes, photographs, names. It's not everything, but it's enough to warrant real attention. We owe it to Annie. And to Carlton, if that's even his real name."

Amelia nodded slowly, her hand pausing around the cup. "We'll go together."

They drove the ten minutes to the Tumblebrook Sheriff's Department in near silence. The building was a squat, redbrick structure that had clearly stood since the '40s, its metal lettering faded and its single flag flapping against a cloudless sky. The parking lot was mostly empty.

Inside, the lobby smelled faintly of stale coffee and worn paper. A ceiling fan turned slowly overhead despite the chill. Behind the reception counter, a tired-looking officer in his late forties glanced up from a clipboard, his badge slightly tarnished, his expression unreadable. He wore the kind of permanent frown that made newcomers feel like troublemakers.

"Farnsworth. Henderson. What can I do for you?"

Clara stepped forward and placed the folder on the counter, her pulse loud in her ears. "We've uncovered some materials connected to the death of Martin Hale. And possibly the disappearance of the man who checked into Room Five under a false name. We believe it's all connected."

The officer blinked, flipping the folder open. "Martin Hale? That's decades old. Why stir all that up again?"

"Because someone doesn't want it stirred," Clara said evenly. "And people are getting hurt."

He skimmed the documents—handwritten notes, the black-and-white photograph, the annotated map. He let out a slow breath through his nose. "This is circumstantial at best. Old stories. Scribbled theories. A missing person who might've just left town. You don't even have his real name."

Amelia leaned in. "He was asking questions. Following a trail. Then he vanished. That should raise concern."

The officer's tone hardened. "I'm not saying it isn't odd. But unless you have something more concrete—evidence of foul play, a suspect, a body—we can't act on this."

Clara clenched her jaw. "You won't even open a case?"

He closed the folder and slid it back across the counter. "We'll make a note of it."

Clara wanted to scream. Instead, she scooped up the folder and said with strained calm, "Thank you for your time."

Outside, the wind whipped through the bare trees and left goosebumps along Clara's arms despite her coat. They stood in silence on the steps for a long moment before Clara turned and started walking. Her frustration spilled from her in short, angry strides. The file trembled in her hands.

They wandered down Main Street, past windows decorated with harvest wreaths and sleepy storefronts. Even in its charm, Tumblebrook seemed to turn its eyes away from them, as if the town itself conspired to forget the truth. The stillness felt performative—like a stage waiting for the curtain to fall.

They reached the café by midmorning. The place was nearly empty, save for Millie Jefferson sitting in her usual corner, nervously stirring her coffee. A half-eaten cranberry muffin sat untouched on her plate, its bright red fruit glistening beneath the dim light.

Clara paused. "She's avoiding us."

Amelia nodded. "She's scared."

But Millie looked up. Her smile faltered, and after a beat of hesitation, she waved them over.

"I heard you went to the police," she said without preamble as they sat.

Clara nodded. "They dismissed it. Didn't even pretend they'd help."

Millie sighed and leaned forward. "Too many people tied to that old mess. Too many reputations resting on the idea that it was just an accident."

Amelia narrowed her eyes. "Millie, why the change? You helped us before."

Millie looked down at her coffee. Her fingers trembled slightly. "Because someone came to see me. Last night. Said it wasn't wise to keep digging. That some things are better left buried. I thought they were just being dramatic... but they knew things. About Annie. About the inn."

Clara's voice was quiet but urgent. "Who was it?"

"I don't know. Tall. Wore a hat. Spoke like someone used to being obeyed. Never gave a name. Just... warned me. Said I'd do well to stay away from the Farnsworth girls and their ghosts."

Amelia bristled. "You think we're making this up?"

"No," Millie said quickly. "But I think you're in danger."

Clara leaned closer. "Millie. Please. Anything you remember— anything—might help."

Millie hesitated, then reached into her purse. "I haven't told anyone else this."

She pulled out a photograph, its edges soft and its colors faded with time. It showed a younger Martin Hale, smiling broadly in front of a cabin framed by pine trees. Around his neck hung a pendant—an oddly shaped talisman with a crescent wrapped in ivy.

"He never took it off," Millie said, her voice far away. "Said it was from his mother. Said it kept him safe in the woods."

Clara squinted at the shape. "We've seen that symbol. On the map."

Amelia whispered, "It was drawn near the site labeled TR #3."

Clara's brow furrowed. "Do you still have it?"

Millie shook her head. "No one saw it after he died. It wasn't in the police report. It just... disappeared."

Just then, Amelia's phone buzzed. A message from Bethany, the inn's receptionist:

You won't believe this. Someone left a strange object on the counter this morning. No note. Looks old. Almost like a charm?

Clara's heart skipped. "Ask her to send a photo."

Seconds later, the image appeared.

The talisman.

Worn. Scratched. Unmistakable.

Millie gasped. "That's it. That's Martin's."

The café suddenly felt colder. The cheery lights above them flickered, and for a heartbeat, the hum of conversation and clinking mugs felt impossibly far away.

Someone had returned it.

Not by accident.

Clara looked to Amelia, whose face had gone pale.

"They're watching us," Clara murmured.

"And they want us to know it," Amelia replied.

Lady Grey, who had trailed behind them and now sat curled under their table, let out a low, distinct chirp. She stood, padded out from under the bench, and walked with purpose toward the café's chalkboard menu.

"What's she doing?" Millie asked.

Clara and Amelia followed.

Lady Grey batted at a few scattered sugar granules on the floor—pawing at them until the motion formed a curved line. Then another. A third.

A pawprint. Then another. Then four in a perfect arc.

"She's drawing something," Clara whispered.

Amelia's eyes widened. "It's the same pattern on the map. The symbol beside the crescent—Lady Grey just traced it."

Millie stepped back, visibly shaken. "She's not just a cat, is she?"

"No," Clara said softly. "She's our compass."

Outside, a delivery truck rumbled past. Inside, the air was thick with realization. Whatever lay at TR #3 was more than buried evidence.

It was a warning. Or a promise.

And someone had just changed the game.

They were no longer chasing a mystery.

They were part of it.

Clara turned back toward Amelia. "We need to go to the map again. Take everything—Annie's journal, the ledger, the photographs. I think we're missing a sequence—something Lady Grey keeps trying to lead us to."

Amelia nodded, her voice quiet. "We'll leave before dawn."

Millie shivered. "Please be careful. There's more danger in those woods than you know."

Lady Grey sat upright, tail curled, eyes locked on the window.

Whatever—or whoever—was coming next had already begun to move.

Chapter 11

Clues in the Talismans

Amelia Farnsworth stood in the study of the Tumblebrook Inn, the talisman cupped delicately in her palm. Morning sunlight streamed through the lace curtains, catching the tarnished metal and making it shimmer faintly. It was heavier than she'd expected, as if the years had infused it with the weight of secrets. The crescent moon motif wrapped in ivy was unmistakable—identical to the symbol drawn in Annie's journal margins, etched into the old cellar box, and now, mysteriously returned. The pendant seemed to hum with silent tension, an object that had borne witness to things most people were never meant to know.

Clara sat at the writing desk, flipping through Annie's journal again, her brow furrowed in concentration. Her fingertips were smudged with ink, and small post-it flags peeked from the pages like whispers pointing toward hidden truths. The journal was no longer just a relic—it had become a guide, a living thread connecting them to the shadowed past. Lady Grey sprawled nearby on the rug, tail twitching in quiet rhythm. The cat's golden eyes flicked between the talisman and the journal with a feline awareness that unnerved and endeared Amelia in equal measure.

"This thing isn't just decorative," Amelia murmured. She turned the pendant over in her hand, revealing a series of faint etchings. Most were worn down, but one symbol stood out: a spiral enclosed in a triangle, with three dots aligned underneath.

Clara leaned in. "That's the same symbol Annie labeled 'Ritual Marking.' I thought it was just symbolic."

"Apparently not." Amelia placed the talisman beside the journal. "Do you think it's tied to the logger's death?"

"I think it's tied to something older," Clara said. "Annie hinted at secret gatherings in the woods. This could've been a token—proof of belonging. Or a warning."

Amelia's thoughts spiraled. She had grown up believing in Tumblebrook's quiet charm and trustworthy traditions. But now, those traditions looked more like disguises. "Let's start at the archives."

Clara nodded, already packing the journal into her bag. "If someone returned this talisman, they're sending a message—or provoking us. Either way, someone's watching."

Lady Grey gave a sharp meow, as if in agreement, then promptly swatted a paperweight off the desk. It clattered to the floor, startling both women.

Amelia chuckled softly. Only Lady Grey could lighten a moment this tense.

* * *

Tumblebrook's historical archives were housed in a converted schoolhouse just off Main Street. Though its red-painted walls had been restored, the interior remained charmingly outdated, its shelves creaking with ledgers, genealogical logs, and forgotten maps. A brass bell jingled as they entered, but no one came to greet them.

The lobby was cool and quiet. Mrs. Durney, the longtime archivist, was missing from her usual post. A half-drunk cup of tea sat cooling beside an open ledger. The stillness felt uneasy. Even the floorboards seemed to hold their breath. The air carried a faint metallic tang—like the scent of old keys and forgotten promises.

"That's odd," Amelia whispered.

Clara scanned the visitor's logbook. No entries for the day. The last had been two days prior, signed in an unfamiliar hand.

They moved deeper into the building, their footsteps muffled by worn rugs. At the back, the oldest records waited. The air turned colder, laced with dust and aging paper. Lady Grey, who had padded in beside them despite the "No Pets" sign, leapt to a windowsill. Her ears twitched at some unseen sound. Her tail flicked once, sharply. A low growl followed—not hostile, but aware.

Amelia found the section marked 1950–1965. "This should cover Martin Hale's death."

Clara scanned nearby labels. "Family land transfers, business permits... Here—civic meeting minutes."

They pulled a leather-bound volume. Inside were handwritten records: council meeting notes, attendance logs, lists of expenditures. Clara flipped carefully through the pages. Amelia helped scan, the silence between them thick.

Clara traced her finger down a March 1959 entry. "Here. Closed meeting on March 17th. No details—just attendees."

Amelia read aloud: "Edgar Harrington. Philip Greaves. Martin Hale."

"He was there," she whispered. "Whatever happened that night— he was part of it."

Clara flipped further, then frowned. "The next month is missing." "What?"

She showed the gap. The March 17th entry was followed by a torn page, then blank sheets until May. "They ripped them out."

Amelia's spine prickled. "They didn't want anyone reading what came next."

Lady Grey leapt down and padded to a filing cabinet behind an armchair. She pawed at it. Clara opened the drawer.

Inside was a bundle of unfiled photographs. Some blurry, others sharp. Town officials, school events...

Then Clara froze. She held up an image taken in the woods. Nighttime. A bonfire burned. Figures stood in a half-circle. On one man's chest: the talisman.

Amelia stared. "That's Edgar Harrington."

"He was wearing it," Clara whispered. "Martin either got it from him—or it was part of something bigger."

She thumbed through the stack. One photo stood out—an overhead forest map with concentric rings and coordinates. On the back: The Hollow—Equinox 1959.

They left the archive with copies of the photos, the map, and more questions than answers. Lady Grey led the way, tail high. The sun dipped westward, casting long shadows across Main Street. The town felt subdued, as if holding a collective breath.

Back at the inn, they spread their findings on the kitchen table. The photo. The journal. The talisman. The map. The table became a mosaic of unearthed truths.

Clara read from Annie's journal: "Symbols recur. Spiral, crescent, triangle. Tied to the equinox. I believe the logger was to meet someone the night of his death. A rendezvous. He never returned."

Amelia exhaled. "It wasn't random. Someone called him out there."

"And whoever it was—wasn't alone."

They sat in silence. Amelia poured tea; the air smelled of chamomile and cedar polish. Clara adjusted the blinds, casting slats of light across the journal. Lady Grey jumped onto a chair, curling neatly, her eyes fixed on the talisman.

Amelia flipped to the next journal page.

A date: September 21, 1959. Beneath it: Meet at the hollow. Bring the proof. Sunset.

Clara whispered, "That's the night Martin died."

Lady Grey leapt onto the table, nudging the talisman until it spun in a slow, deliberate circle. Its shadow danced across the wood. The ticking kitchen clock grew thunderous.

Their next destination was clear.

But the past—so carefully hidden—was stirring once more.

Chapter 12

Reconstructing the Past

Clara Henderson leaned over the reference desk in the Tumblebrook Library, a stack of microfiche printouts fanned beside her like cards in an unsolved hand. Her eyes, tired but focused, scanned each paragraph of a decades-old obituary with the practiced precision of someone who had spent too many nights searching for answers in places others had forgotten. Dust motes danced lazily in the shafts of light streaming through the tall windows, giving the room a cathedral-like reverence. The microfilm reader hummed softly—the quiet machinery of history grinding against time's forgetfulness.

The subject was Martin Hale—the logger whose death had, until recently, been considered a closed chapter in Tumblebrook's long and quiet history. But that version of events had begun to crumble. The questions now came faster than the answers, like dominoes toppling through a field of silence.

She took a sip of lukewarm coffee and reached for the next slip. The paper was brittle at the edges, the ink faded but intact. This obituary was from the local newspaper, but she'd found the same words copied—oddly word-for-word—in the Consortium's internal newsletters. Far too scripted to be natural.

"Martin Hale, 32, beloved son of Ruth and Gerald Hale, passed unexpectedly in September of 1959..." Clara skimmed ahead. Nothing about foul play. Nothing even remotely suspicious. But there it was again—buried in the list of mourners: E.H.

"Edgar Harrington," she whispered, her pen halting mid-sentence.

She pulled out the slip she'd marked earlier, a snippet from a 1957 town hall ledger: "Property dispute regarding the Pine Hollow tract escalated between M. Hale and E. Harrington..."

So they had a history. Hale wasn't just a victim of circumstance; he'd been in direct opposition to one of the town's most powerful men. She jotted a note beside the clipping, underlining the words: Land rights. Hostility. Pattern of interference?

As she combed through more materials, a fuller picture of Martin Hale began to emerge. He wasn't just a logger. He'd been a local advocate—attending council meetings, submitting complaints to the forestry department, even organizing informal protests against illegal logging. There were letters to the editor of the Tumblebrook Herald, each bearing his name and a scathing tone toward misused permits and suspicious land transfers. The deeper Clara dug, the clearer it became: Hale had made enemies. Influential ones.

She unearthed more than expected. A handwritten complaint dated August 1958 described a nighttime confrontation between Hale and two unnamed men on the Pine Hollow tract—reported by a neighbor who later recanted the statement. Another article mentioned that Hale had attempted to run for a council seat but was rejected due to "procedural errors." He appeared to be a man determined to fight for fairness—and others equally determined to stop him.

She turned her attention to archived photos. Black-and-white images showed Hale with protest signs, surrounded by townsfolk at campfires, meeting in church basements, standing at the front of town gatherings. Clara lingered over one photo in particular—Hale and a young woman with familiar eyes. Annie. They stood shoulder to shoulder, defiant.

Clara carefully scanned meeting minutes and land deed logs. She highlighted more discrepancies—ownership documents that vanished from one year to the next, parcels that changed hands suspiciously fast, and a recurring signature she didn't recognize: W.B. Possibly a middleman. The scale of the deceit was larger than she'd imagined.

The library's lights flickered overhead as the wind howled outside. Clara checked her watch. Nearly noon.

She packed her bag, heart racing with the weight of her discoveries, and stepped out into the blustery afternoon. The wind whipped leaves around her boots as she made her way down Main Street. Tumblebrook's charm had dulled—its painted windows and cobbled sidewalks now seemed to veil a deeper rot.

Back at the inn, the front desk bell chimed as she entered.

"Clara?" Amelia's voice drifted from the parlor. "You'll want to hear this."

Clara set her bag down and joined Amelia, who was seated with a guest Clara hadn't seen before—a woman in her late forties with dark-rimmed glasses, smart attire, and the alert gaze of someone used to confidentiality.

"This is Nadine Harker," Amelia said. "She's in Room Eight. Used to work for the North Shore Timber Consortium."

Clara's brows lifted.

Nadine offered a tight smile. "Until I became... expendable. Legal division. Contracts and acquisitions. But some files were too dirty to ignore. I started asking questions. You know how that goes."

Clara sat. "What kind of files?"

"Logging permits. Land evaluations. Transfers made without full council knowledge. It wasn't sloppy. It was calculated."

Amelia folded her hands. "And Martin Hale?"

"He protested the land deals. He knew Pine Hollow was part of a conservation grant—not open to commercial use. But Harrington had pull. The documents vanished. Replaced, or buried."

Clara looked to Amelia. "So he was in the way."

Nadine nodded. "And someone made sure he didn't stand long."

Even Lady Grey, nestled near the fire, paused her grooming to glance toward them.

"Why now?" Clara asked. "Why speak up?"

"Because it's happening again," Nadine said. "Different names. Same hands. They've just gotten better at hiding it."

Clara felt the chill down to her bones. This wasn't just history. It was prophecy.

After Nadine excused herself, Amelia poured fresh tea and stared into the fire. Shadows danced across the floorboards.

"It's not just the past," she said. "It's still happening."

Clara nodded. "And they want us to fold early."

Lady Grey stretched, yawned, and wandered to the writing table. She pawed at a scrap of torn paper, flipping it.

Clara bent to retrieve it. A flyer. The header read: Save Our Forest—Town Meeting October 1958. The edges were scorched.

"A rally," Amelia said. "Annie mentioned it."

"It was real," Clara replied. "And they tried to erase it."

The flyer included a partial list of signatures. One stood out—M. Hale. Another bore the faded initials A.F.

"Could be Annie," Clara said, heart pounding.

At the bottom of the page, in pencil: Trust no minutes. Truth lives in the margins.

That evening, Clara returned to her room as dusk fell. She laid out everything on her bed—articles, annotations, the journal, the flyer. Then she opened her satchel.

A letter. Folded. Unmarked.

She hadn't put it there.

Hands trembling, she opened it. The paper smelled faintly of cedar. The handwriting was precise, oddly elegant:

You've walked too far into waters deeper than you understand. Stop swimming. Before you sink.

No name. No address. Just a warning.

Clara stared at the note, her breath shallow. Someone had been in her room.

Lady Grey appeared in the doorway. Her amber eyes locked with Clara's, then shifted to the flyer on the bed. Without a sound, the cat leapt up, curled beside it, and rested her head as if standing guard.

Clara whispered, to no one in particular, "We're not done yet. Not even close."

Chapter 13

The Gathering Storm

Amelia Farnsworth stood at the front window of the Tumblebrook Inn, arms crossed as she watched gray clouds roll low over the lake. The sky had taken on a strange greenish hue—ominous, like it was holding its breath. A storm was coming. Not just the one rumbling in the sky, but something deeper, older, and far more dangerous. She could feel it—like the air before lightning. The wind carried a strange texture, a heaviness that hinted at more than weather. Her fingertips grazed the cold glass, and for a moment, she imagined she could touch the edges of the truth now circling them like carrion birds.

Lady Grey perched on the windowsill, tail twitching with each gust. The cat had been unusually restless all morning, slipping in and out of rooms, pausing to paw at doorjambs or stare at nothing. That always meant something. Her instincts were rarely wrong, and Amelia had learned to trust them. If the cat was unsettled, something was coming.

She turned as Clara entered from the parlor, a stack of notes tucked under her arm. Behind her came Millie Jefferson, her bright scarf flapping in the wind like a banner of defiance. Millie's cheeks were pink from the cold, and though her stride had slowed over the years, it still carried purpose. She looked every bit the formidable matriarch of Tumblebrook's oral history. Amelia felt comforted—and steeled—by her presence.

"We're all here," Amelia said, motioning for them to gather in the private sitting room she reserved for important guests. Today, it served a higher purpose. The room carried the scent of old wood polish and cinnamon from a simmering pot on the stove—a small comfort.

Millie eased into the armchair by the fireplace. "Heavens, this weather's got my joints howling. But I figure we've got more to worry about than rheumatism."

Clara sat across from her and opened the journal on the coffee table. "We're closing in. But the closer we get, the more dangerous it feels. Nadine's account lines up with everything Annie recorded—land fraud, forged permits, old alliances. But we're still missing the who and the why behind Martin Hale's death. And Annie's silence."

Amelia nodded. "Which is why we need to go to them."

"To the Harringtons?" Clara asked.

"To the entire family," Amelia confirmed. "We have just enough now to ask questions they can't ignore. Maybe even shake something loose."

Millie adjusted her shawl. "You do realize they're not going to invite us in for tea and lemon cake, right? That family's been untouchable since before the mill was built."

"But they're not infallible," Amelia said. "Not with the documents Clara found and Nadine's testimony."

Millie's eyes narrowed. For a moment, Amelia saw a flicker of steel beneath the wrinkles. "If you're going to poke the bear, you'd better know how to run."

"Then help us build a map of where to run," Clara said. "We need everything you remember. Every story. Even the gossip."

Millie sighed, then leaned back. "The Harringtons always had a reputation. Sharp as foxes, just as cunning. Edgar's father—old Royce

Harrington—ran half the town from behind a desk at the lumber yard. Folks said he bought up a family farm just to tear it down and plant white pines. Claimed it helped the timber trade, but rumor had it he found something buried under the barn."

"Buried?" Amelia echoed.

Millie shrugged. "No one ever said what. Gold, bones, who knows. But after that, the farm was off-limits. Deed stayed in his name until the day he died."

Clara jotted notes. "Where was the farm?"

"West Hollow Road. Near the creek. What's left of it burned in the '60s."

"Did Annie ever talk about it?" Amelia asked.

Millie hesitated. "She did. Said the fire wasn't an accident. I didn't think much of it then. Annie saw danger where others didn't."

"That was her gift," Amelia said. "She saw what needed remembering."

A log snapped in the fireplace, sending a flash of sparks into the grate. All three women turned toward the sound, as if summoned by tension.

Lady Grey jumped down from the window and padded toward the hallway, ears flat. She let out a low, steady growl.

Amelia moved to the hallway and peeked around the corner. The front door was locked. Curtains drawn. Nothing out of place. She listened. Heart pounding.

Then came the unmistakable creak of floorboards in the kitchen.

Amelia turned back to the others, holding a finger to her lips. She moved toward the kitchen, Lady Grey a silent shadow at her side.

She pushed open the swinging door. No one. But something had changed. A dish towel lay on the floor. A cabinet hung open. One of the back windows was unlatched. The breeze that drifted in smelled of rain on rust. And cologne—unfamiliar, sharp.

On the center island was a piece of folded parchment.

Amelia approached. The paper was thick, yellowed. She opened it and read:

I know the truth about Annie. She didn't fall silent. She was silenced. Meet me. Midnight. The boathouse.

Thunder cracked. The wind moaned under the eaves. Amelia's stomach turned. Not in fear—in anticipation.

She turned to the hallway, note in hand. Clara and Millie waited, their faces tense.

"Someone was here," Amelia said. "And they left this."

Clara read the note. "The handwriting is unfamiliar. But it sounds like someone who knows exactly what Annie was doing."

"We should be cautious," Millie said. "Plenty would use that kind of bait for a trap."

Amelia looked at the clock. Just past five. Midnight loomed.

"I want to meet them," she said. "But we plan. We observe. And we don't go alone."

Clara nodded. "We take shifts watching the boathouse from the shore. If someone shows up early, we'll know."

"And I'll pack something heavier than a flashlight," Millie muttered.

For the next hour, they laid out maps of the lake. Amelia spread the boathouse floorplan from an old brochure; Clara used topographic charts to mark high ground. They mapped fallback points, communication signals, and what to do if separated. Flashlight signals: two for danger, three for safe passage.

Lady Grey stayed close, curling in corners, flicking her tail. Every now and then, she glanced toward the kitchen.

Amelia lit more candles around the inn. Their flames flickered wildly in the drafts. The wind howled outside. A shutter slammed somewhere out back.

As twilight deepened and the lamps glowed warm against the storm, Amelia felt the full weight of the night ahead settle over her. What came next wouldn't just test their resolve—it might upend the fragile balance Tumblebrook had clung to for decades.

She checked the note again.

Midnight. Not just a time now. A countdown.

Chapter 14

Harrowing Hideaway

Rain fell in relentless sheets as Clara Henderson huddled beneath her coat, boots squelching along the muddy path that led to the old boathouse tucked behind the reeds at the lake's edge. The trail twisted through wild thickets and half-drowned cattails, guiding her toward the wooden structure that loomed in the mist like a relic from another age. The air was thick with damp earth and memory, charged with the sharp scent of wet pine and decaying leaves. Every gust of wind seemed to carry secrets long buried beneath the lake's surface—secrets now inching their way back to the light.

She clutched Annie Farnsworth's journal to her chest, heart pounding with a sense of urgency that pushed her forward despite the storm. The pages inside were fragile, but the words burned in her mind. This place, this boathouse, had witnessed something monumental. And now it was calling them back. Each of Annie's entries unfolded with eerie clarity, each detail imbued with purpose.

Behind her, Amelia Farnsworth followed closely, flashlight beam bobbing with each careful step. Her coat flapped against her legs, heavy with rain. Lady Grey padded ahead, unbothered by the wet ground, drawn by something unseen. Her presence was steadying, a quiet reassurance that they were on the right path. The wind tugged at Amelia's hood, carrying whispers through the trees. For a moment, Clara could almost believe the town itself was urging them forward. They had reached the point of no return. Whatever waited at the boathouse would change everything.

The boathouse emerged through the curtain of rain, its silhouette jagged and worn. Shingles were missing from the roof, and planks curled outward like loose teeth. The structure sagged beneath its own weight, yet radiated an undeniable gravity—the kind that came from secrets sealed in wood and silence. Moss clung to the siding like forgotten fingerprints. Clara reached for the iron latch, slick with rain, and pushed.

The door creaked open on rusted hinges. The air inside was close and heavy, thick with mildew, lakewater, and something else—the scent of old paper, oil, and time. A single lantern flickered in the center of the room, casting long shadows across warped floorboards, dust-covered crates, and the remnants of nets and fishing gear. Cobwebs sagged in the corners like weary guardians. Water plinked steadily from beams above.

Clara stepped inside first, eyes sharp. She could feel it—this place had once held whispers, arguments, secrets passed in haste. The walls seemed to breathe in the darkness, listening still. Everything about the space whispered danger and unfinished business. She ran her hand along a post, splinters catching her glove.

"This was it," Clara murmured. "The place Annie wrote about. This is where she met someone. Someone she never named."

Amelia closed the door, muffling the storm. She propped the flashlight on a beam, casting its glow across the room. Lady Grey leapt onto a wooden bench in the corner and sat regally, amber eyes tracking every movement. Her gaze fixed on the far end of the boathouse, as if she remembered something no one else could.

They moved in silence, each step heavy with anticipation. Clara ran her fingers along an old worktable coated in dust. Carved into the surface were initials: E.H.

"Edgar Harrington," she said, barely above a breath.

Amelia knelt beside her and traced the letters. "He used this place. As a meeting point, maybe. Or something more permanent. A hideout."

Clara opened Annie's journal to the last entry they'd deciphered:

He said the lake had always been a mirror—it shows you what you bring to it. I didn't understand until I saw what floated beneath the floorboards.

As if summoned by the words, Lady Grey gave a low, rumbling meow and padded to the far end of the boathouse, where the floor dipped slightly and the boards appeared recently disturbed. She brushed aside a cobweb with her tail, revealing a narrow gap between planks. She scratched at the corner.

Clara and Amelia knelt to inspect. Clara pressed her palm to a board that groaned under her weight. With care, they pried it up, revealing a hollow beneath. A rusted metal box sat within, its corners mottled with corrosion but sealed. It smelled of oil and decay, like time folded inside.

Clara held her breath and opened it.

Inside were photographs. Grainy, black-and-white images of Martin Hale. One showed him standing on the dock outside, gesturing intensely. Another showed him with a young man Clara recognized as a junior officer from the archives. A third photo was torn in half—only half a face remained, but it resembled a young Edgar Harrington.

Beneath the photographs were folded letters. Weathered pages filled with tight, slanted handwriting. Notes. A map. And at the bottom, a gold pin engraved with the monarch emblem.

They sat in stunned silence, the rain echoing like a drumbeat of discovery. Amelia held one letter to the lantern.

"It says the logger had evidence—financial records, land surveys, testimonies. Enough to expose the land deal completely. This letter warns him not to speak at the festival. Tells him to stay away from the boathouse."

Clara leaned over her shoulder. The ink was faded but legible. The handwriting was elegant and chillingly calm. The letter was unsigned. More pages revealed details about payments, initials of collaborators, and dates matching mysterious town events.

They turned page after page, uncovering betrayal. Names. Dates. Coded references. Clara's hands trembled as she held a yellowed map marked with the oak tree emblem. Marginalia hinted at meeting sites, payment drops, and signals. A conspiracy, decades long—and possibly still active.

"They were more organized than we thought," Amelia whispered. "This wasn't just a power grab. It was a system."

Lady Grey hissed suddenly, her back arched. She stared at the window.

Clara and Amelia turned.

A shadow passed across the frosted glass—tall, slow-moving. It paused. Then vanished.

Amelia grabbed the flashlight. Clara snatched the box and journal. Amelia extinguished the lantern.

They crouched in the dark, breath held tight.

Footsteps outside. Then nothing. Just the wind.

Minutes passed. The silence roared. Thunder cracked.

"We have to leave," Clara whispered.

Amelia nodded. "Now."

They slipped through the door and darted into the storm, soaked but clutching the proof. Evidence someone had tried to bury—and someone was still trying.

Lady Grey, calm and deliberate, led them through the rain, her tail flicking against the wind. The inn's distant lights flickered through the mist. Clara gripped the journal tighter, knowing every answer sharpened the questions ahead.

They didn't speak as they walked.
They didn't need to.
The truth, long buried, was speaking for itself.

Chapter 15

Truth in the Shadows

Clara Henderson sat at the long oak dining table in the inn's quiet common room, her notebook splayed open and filled with dense lines of handwriting, looping arrows across timelines, and margins scribbled with hurried questions and half-formed theories. Outside, the storm had risen into a ferocious chorus, hammering the windows with wind-driven rain and battering the eaves like a warning drumbeat. Late autumn air seeped through even the thickest curtains, carrying the raw scent of earth and electricity. The windows moaned in their frames as if protesting the weight of the weather. The fire in the hearth snapped occasionally, casting jittery shadows that danced across the paneled walls like ghosts trying to speak.

Beside her, a mug of coffee had long gone cold—her third of the day, poured with hope and abandoned once she slipped into a trance of discovery. She barely noticed time anymore. Her world had narrowed to ink, parchment, and the ghostly echoes of long-buried truths. Her shoulders ached from hours hunched over the journal and her own increasingly frantic notes. Her eyes, rimmed with fatigue, flicked constantly between papers, charts, and theories that stretched like veins across the table. The rain added its own rhythm to the hush of the room, and deeper in the inn, the wood groaned like it was remembering.

Lady Grey dozed near the hearth, tail curled neatly, one ear twitching with each shift of the house. Earlier, the cat had stared into the shadows for a solid hour—fixated, ears flicking, eyes narrowed. It wasn't Clara's imagination. Lady Grey was sensing something. Something alive, or perhaps just long-forgotten and now restless. Clara felt it too. They weren't just observers anymore. They were part of something decades in the making. The storm only deepened that suspicion —as though Tumblebrook itself was warning them.

The box from the boathouse had been emptied onto the table like the bones of some long-dead creature. Clara had sorted the photographs, letters, and coded maps with meticulous care. Martin Hale's photograph—captured mid-gesture on the dock—stared up from a protective plastic sleeve. Beside it lay the torn image of Edgar Harrington, its jagged edge like a wound.

The monarch pin sat in a dish near Annie's journal—its symbolism now clear. Clara had traced the Monarch Society through at least ten separate documents recovered beneath the floorboards. The map included cross-referenced meeting points, matching symbols from Annie's journal, and a series of dates aligning with odd newspaper clippings Amelia had unearthed the year before.

She flipped through her notes, watching patterns emerge. Royce Harrington. Edgar Harrington. Martin Hale. Dozens of deeds, property transfers, and unexplained disputes now connected by lines that intersected with uncanny precision. Millie's stories—once harmless folklore—had become damning testimony. Clara traced her finger along the timeline. 1955: Pine Hollow acquisition. 1957: land dispute. 1959: Harvest Festival. 1960: the fire. A sequence not of coincidence but of orchestration and erasure.

She turned again to Annie's journal:

"At the autumn fair, he stood tall and accused them—said no

amount of trees could cover the truth. But no one answered. They turned away. Pretended it didn't happen. Later, he was gone. Just like that."

That moment—public, loud, and surrounded by witnesses—had become a vortex in Clara's research. What had Martin revealed? How could a whole town swallow the story of an accident? How could an entire crowd remain silent? Clara imagined the faces of those in 1959—some shocked, some indifferent, some terrified. How many had knowingly chosen to forget?

She retrieved the fragile flyer from Annie's box:

Tumblebrook Harvest Festival — September 19, 1959. Parade at 11 a.m. — Open Mic at 2 p.m. — Evening Bonfire 7:00.

If Martin had spoken at the microphone, his voice had echoed across the hillside. And someone had decided he wouldn't speak again. The fairgrounds, once vibrant, had been left to rot, erased by time. That date—no longer just a line on a page—was the epicenter.

Lady Grey rose and trotted to the bay window, posture tense. Ears forward. Tail flicking like a metronome.

Clara followed her gaze. Through the fog and rain, the hill behind the inn loomed. Trees stood in unnatural patterns. Clara realized the layout had once been intentional—pathways, now swallowed by root and moss.

She stood, wrapped herself in her wool coat, and slipped out the back door. The cold stung her cheeks. Rain trickled down her neck. Her boots squelched into the sodden grass. Each step felt like an unspoken vow. Lady Grey followed, graceful and silent.

Halfway up the hill, the storm eased into a steady drizzle. The clearing opened in a ghostly flash of lightning. They found it near a tree stump: rusted stakes, shards of pottery, sun-bleached ribbon.

Clara brushed away the soil. A plaque emerged:

Harvest Pavilion — Donated 1946

She took photos. Then saw it: a rusted badge tangled in bramble. On the back—E.H.

Back at the inn, soaked and breathless, she dropped her coat and raced to the table. She cross-referenced the badge with Annie's journal. A line jumped out:

"He wore the badge to hide behind it. They said he was fair security. But he was watching everyone."

Clara's skin prickled. Edgar Harrington hadn't just been present. He had orchestrated it.

She stood, ready to find Millie, when Amelia entered, pale.

"It's gone," she whispered. "The emergency radios. The satellite phone. Generator pack. Even the lanterns."

Clara froze. "What? How?"

"No forced entry. No tripped sensors. Just... gone."

They swept through the inn, checking locks, doors, windows. Lady Grey padded silently beside them.

Clara re-threaded copper bells along doors and handrails. Millie arrived, arms full of furniture to barricade the side entrances. The three women moved in focused silence, fear sharpening their coordination.

"We're being cornered," Clara said.

"Someone doesn't want the truth getting out," Amelia replied. "And they're willing to play dirty."

In the parlor, Clara lit candles and opened Annie's journal. The fire crackled. Shadows moved like restless spirits. The journal's spine creaked as she flattened it.

New ink smudges.

A fresh passage:

"The truth they buried is rising like floodwater. If it reaches the surface, it'll drown the town. But if it stays buried, it'll rot us from within."

Lady Grey leapt into her lap. Her warmth grounded Clara.

Amelia returned with tea. Her voice was steady.

"We're in it now. No walking back."

Clara nodded, eyes fixed on the badge atop Annie's notes, beside the butterfly pin and the map.

"We dig until the last secret is out."
Outside, the wind howled.
And somewhere in the dark, someone listened.

Chapter 16

Whispers in the Wind

Amelia Farnsworth stood at the rain-blurred window of the Tumblebrook Inn's upper parlor, the morning light dimmed to a bruised gray by the heavy clouds. Though the worst of the storm had passed in the night, the town outside remained cloaked in an eerie silence, broken only by the occasional caw of a raven or the distant rattle of wind through the bare trees. Her hands, wrapped around a chipped porcelain teacup, were steady, but inside, her mind raced.

The disappearance of the guest—Mr. Carlton Maddox—and the discovery of blackmail notes hidden beneath the floorboards of the boathouse had shifted something in Amelia. No longer could she pretend this investigation was just about uncovering an old mystery. The truth had claws. It was tearing through generations, scratching at Tumblebrook's carefully maintained veneer. The box they uncovered in the boathouse had made everything real—names, connections, and motives that had slept for decades, waiting to be unearthed. Every page in Annie's journal, every trinket and note they found, now echoed louder.

Carlton Maddox had listed a contact upon check-in: an older

man named Giles Rourke who lived on the outskirts of town in a former park ranger's cabin. Amelia made the decision to visit him immediately, despite the foul weather and Clara's concern about venturing out. The storm might have passed, but the tension around the inn had not. It hung in the air like static, waiting to snap. Lady Grey had been particularly unsettled that morning, darting from room to room, pausing near the inn's western wall as if sensing something beyond what Amelia could grasp. Her instincts had proven right more times than not.

By midmorning, she and Clara were bumping along a rutted forest road in Amelia's old pickup. Lady Grey was nestled in a crate in the backseat, yowling her protest at every jolt. Trees crowded the road's edge, their bare limbs reaching like skeletal arms toward the windshield. The sky remained a slate-colored dome overhead, giving the illusion of perpetual dusk. Clara tapped a finger against her notebook, reviewing the timeline again.

"Giles was Maddox's mentor in environmental law," she said aloud. "If anyone knew what Maddox was working on, it's him."

Amelia nodded. "And we need to know if Maddox was on to something... something that got him silenced. We can't afford another missing piece."

The truck rattled as they crossed a wooden bridge slick with rain, water rushing beneath in swollen torrents. Birds scattered as they approached the cabin, which stood weather-beaten but sturdy, its dark wood blending with the trees. Moss crept up the base of the porch, and an old rocking chair creaked faintly in the wind.

Giles Rourke opened the door after a long pause. He was in his late seventies, with silver hair and the tall, lean frame of someone who had spent a lifetime outdoors. His eyes were sharp behind square glasses. He greeted them with narrowed eyes and a wary tone.

"Carlton's missing?"

"Since yesterday," Amelia said. "We think he may have been digging into old land records. Ones connected to the Harringtons. And a man named Martin Hale."

At the mention of Hale, Giles went still. His fingers tightened around the doorframe. Then he gestured for them to come inside.

The interior of the cabin was dimly lit, the scent of cedar smoke and old paper lingering in the air. Antique maps adorned the walls alongside framed photos of a younger Giles posing with rangers and field surveyors. It felt like stepping back in time.

"I told Carlton to stay away from this town's history," Giles said as he poured them bitter tea. "It's not just old grudges and unsolved deaths. It's a legacy of control. You dig too deep, and you risk bringing it all down on yourself."

He led them to a desk cluttered with papers. From a locked drawer, he pulled out a slim folder, its edges worn and its contents thick with dust and old secrets. Inside were annotated articles, legal briefs, and one document in particular—a copy of a deed bearing the signature of Martin Hale, alongside a ledger note referencing Pine Hollow Holdings.

"Carlton said he found proof that Martin Hale was involved in more than just timber disputes. He said Hale may have been black-mailing someone powerful. Something about a ledger. But he never told me who."

Clara exchanged a glance with Amelia. "There was a ledger," she said. "We found part of it. And a map. In the boathouse, buried under the floor. There were initials—E.H."

Amelia leaned forward. "Do you know anything about a woman Martin Hale was involved with? Someone the town never acknowledged?"

Giles hesitated. "Only rumors. That she was from the coast. Never married. Had money. And a temper. That's all Carlton could dig up."

He paused, then added, "There was talk of letters. Love notes, maybe. But they disappeared after Hale died. Some say they were burned. Others say someone collected them. He said the woman—Eliza, I think—was a threat to the Harringtons' grip on the town."

They left with more questions than answers, but the visit

confirmed what they had feared: Martin Hale had known something damning, and someone had made sure it disappeared with him.

As Amelia guided the truck back toward the inn, she kept one eye on the forest, wondering who might be watching. The branches above them seemed to shift unnaturally in the wind, like silent witnesses to a truth they weren't ready to name.

Back at the inn, Lady Grey was unusually restless. As Amelia opened the front door, the cat bolted past them, claws clicking across the floorboards. She leapt onto the side table near the front desk and swiped a pale cream envelope to the floor with a hiss.

"What in the—" Clara started.

Lady Grey tore at the envelope with alarming determination until the seal gave way, scattering its contents. Inside were several handwritten letters on delicate stationery, their ink faded but legible. Amelia bent to pick one up and read aloud:

"My Dearest M— I cannot bear the secrecy much longer. Your promises sustain me, but I fear you will choose duty over love. If they find out what we've shared, the consequences will be deadly. Forever Yours, E."

Clara exhaled sharply. "E. As in... Edgar?"

"Or Eliza," Amelia said. "Remember Millie mentioned a woman with that name who vanished from the guesthouse registry in 1959?"

They spread the letters out across the table. One included a passage that matched Annie's handwriting, copied and underlined:

"They warned him the festival would be his last chance to stay silent."

It was the same phrasing used in the boathouse letters. The pieces were clicking into place. Clara began taking photographs, documenting the contents meticulously. The letters painted a picture of desperation, longing, and danger. If Eliza had truly loved Martin, then her silence might have been forced, not chosen. It raised a haunting question: had she paid a price too?

That evening, the town held a seasonal gathering at the community hall. It was an annual potluck, now diminished in spirit but still attended by those who clung to tradition. Clara and Amelia decided to attend, sensing it might offer a chance to gauge the public mood—and possibly send a subtle signal.

The room was crowded with familiar faces. Millie waved them over to a table near the window, but Amelia noticed hushed voices and averted glances as they passed. The town was buzzing. They could feel it like a current in the air. Conversations stopped just as they walked past. Dishes clattered, and smiles fell a little too fast into silence.

Clara whispered, "Do you think someone found out about the boathouse?"

"Someone knew before we did," Amelia replied. "We're not chasing shadows anymore. We're being hunted."

They stayed long enough to speak quietly with a few trusted allies: Mr. Lark from the bookstore, Doris from the café, and even Ezra the reclusive artist, who only nodded once when Clara showed him the butterfly pin. Each reaction confirmed what they suspected: the Monarch Society hadn't disappeared. It had simply gone underground.

As they stepped outside, the sky rumbled ominously. A thick black line of clouds loomed in the distance, advancing fast. The wind that had been whispering all day now turned bold, tugging at coats and hair. A fresh chill swept over them, more biting than before. The air had that uncanny weight again—the heaviness that preceded not just a storm, but something fateful.

Then Amelia's phone buzzed. A message. No number.

Storm coming. You won't be safe tonight. Leave the inn. Now.

She showed Clara. "We need to go. Now."

Lady Grey meowed sharply at their feet, eyes wide, as if confirming the threat. Her fur stood on end. She darted toward the parlor and stared back at them, as if willing them to follow. Her pupils were huge, reflecting the flicker of the outdoor lanterns.

Lightning cracked across the horizon, closer than expected. The wind howled, carrying with it a sound like a scream swallowed by distance. The trees swayed, groaning under invisible pressure. It felt less like weather and more like a reckoning. The tension coiled in their stomachs like wire, brittle and waiting to snap.

And above them, the wind began to whisper again—but this time, it carried words they could almost understand.

Chapter 17

Nature's Reckoning

The storm's second wave hit with a vengeance.

By nightfall, the sky over Tumblebrook cracked open like a torn canvas, spilling rain in sheets and hurling gales that bent even the stubbornest pines. Clara Henderson peered through the inn's fogged windowpane, her breath leaving streaks across the glass as she squinted into the darkness. The lake, which earlier had rippled like a troubled mirror, now churned with frothy waves that slapped against the dock with manic force. Trees groaned beneath the assault, their limbs flailing like frightened dancers.

The weather had turned biblical. Wind screeched down from the hills like a banshee, rattling shutters, lifting loose shingles, and dragging the scent of wet bark and torn roots through every crack in the inn's timbered frame. Rainwater ran in rivulets down the stone path to the front porch, swirling around flowerpots and forgotten boots. Nature had unleashed a fury that felt deeply personal, as if the storm itself were offended by the truths Amelia and Clara had uncovered. Somewhere, a shutter banged repeatedly against the siding—each clang a chilling reminder of how alone they were.

Thunder rolled across the hills, louder and longer than before. It shook the bones of the inn and flickered the lanterns they had spread throughout the downstairs rooms. The power had been out since late afternoon. The landlines, too, had gone dead. Even Amelia's emergency satellite phone had sputtered into silence by dinnertime, its final blinking light fading like a last heartbeat. There were no more lifelines, no more signals. Just the sound of the wind—and the knowledge that they were truly, utterly isolated.

They were cut off.

The inn, so often a haven of comfort and warmth, now stood like a ship adrift in a storm of secrets and wind. Clara stood in the parlor, arms folded tightly across her chest, her notebook pressed to her ribs as if it could shield her from the growing sense of dread. She had spent the last hour cross-referencing Annie's journal with the ledgers from the office, searching for clues that might piece together the puzzle they'd uncovered. Every minute added pressure, and the storm outside seemed to match the rising tension within.

Millie had lit the last of the beeswax candles, setting them in saucers across the kitchen, stairwell, and entryway. Their flickering glow painted shadows across the walls, echoing the ghost stories they'd all heard growing up—about haunted woods and voices on the wind. But this wasn't a ghost story. Not anymore.

This was a reckoning.

"We should track our exits," Clara said, placing her notebook on the dining table and flipping to a hand-drawn map of Tumblebrook. "If they come for us tonight, we need to know where we can run."

Amelia stood beside the hearth, rubbing warmth back into her fingers. "There's the woods to the north. Old hiking paths that loop around the bluff and lead to the stone quarry. But they'll be muddy and dangerous in this weather."

Millie grunted as she adjusted a kettle over the fire. "The logging trail's worse. It turns to soup when it rains. You'll sink to your knees before you hit the first ridge."

Lady Grey paced near the pantry, ears twitching every time the wind howled against the old shutters. She had been uneasy all day, her usual poise replaced by a stalking intensity that reminded Clara of the time the cat had sensed a gas leak before anyone else had noticed a thing. Clara had long since stopped dismissing the feline's instincts.

"We'll note all the trails," Clara said, scribbling notes furiously. "But we need to stay put for now. We have enough food. Wood for the fire. We need to hold out until the weather clears—or until someone slips up."

They spread a large map across the dining table, the corners weighed down with coffee mugs and candlesticks. It was a copy of an older forest survey Annie had tucked away in the journal, filled with annotations in faded ink. Paths, old ranger stations, even forgotten logging cabins were marked. Clara traced the routes with her finger, memorizing the curves, the choke points, the places they could be trapped—or concealed. The map became a battlefield, every red X a skirmish point in a war they hadn't asked to fight.

The three women gathered around the large oak table. On it were the items from the boathouse: the letters, the badge with E.H. etched on its underside, Annie's journal, and a now-wrinkled map with red circles scrawled in haste. Clara pulled the map closer, angling it toward the candlelight.

"I think this mark," she said, tapping a faint X beneath a hill ridge, "is tied to the underground access tunnel mentioned in the festival planning notes. Annie believed Martin Hale had intended to use it as an escape route—maybe to meet Eliza."

"But he never made it," Amelia murmured. "Someone cut him off."

"Or lured him there," Millie added darkly.

The fire popped, sending a spiral of sparks toward the hearth grate. It was the only sound besides the groan of the wind. Clara leaned back and studied the badge again. Edgar Harrington had played the part of event security. Which meant he had keys, sched-ules, access. He could have orchestrated anything under the guise of logistics. Her stomach tightened as she considered the possibilities.

"If we could link Edgar to the financier," Clara said, "the one behind the land grabs and the logging corruption, we could break this whole thing open. All the money trails vanish into shell corporations, but the ledgers we found hinted at a master investor with initials 'H.F.' That's the name we need."

Amelia stood and retrieved a battered shoebox from the inn's office. Inside were old inn ledgers, many of which had belonged to her great aunt Annie. Clara's fingers trembled slightly as she lifted out one labeled Guest Payments, 1958–1961.

"We've searched these before," Amelia said. "But only for names tied directly to the night of the Harvest Festival."

"Let's try a different angle," Clara said. "Recurring payments. Deposits made off-season. Anything unusual. Guests who stayed more than once."

They spent the next hour combing through the ledgers by firelight. Clara's heart thudded with every page. There was something sacred in the silence between them, in the way the shadows danced around Lady Grey as she sat perched on a windowsill, keeping watch. It felt like time folded inward, as though Annie herself stood over their shoulders, guiding their fingers along the paper.

Then Amelia stilled.

"Here. Look."

She pointed to an entry dated March 3, 1959.

Deposit from H. Fawcett – private room, no meals requested, three nights.

Millie's eyes narrowed. "Fawcett. That name's not in the town registry."

"But it's on the guestbook," Amelia said. "And not just once. Two more times. Always off-season. Always with the same initials."

Clara scribbled furiously in her notebook. "If H. Fawcett was the financier—possibly hiding behind that name—he could've been staying here to oversee operations. Quietly. Behind the scenes."

"Which means Annie knew," Millie added. "And she logged it all."

Lady Grey, as if stirred by their discovery, leapt off the windowsill and padded across the room. She stopped at a bookshelf near the hearth, pawed once at the bottom shelf, and sat down.

Clara tilted her head. "She's found something."

Amelia knelt and pulled out a dusty volume. But the shelf didn't sit flush with the wall. When she pressed against the back panel, a soft click echoed.

A hidden compartment.

Inside was a rolled-up scroll, tied with a thin ribbon and stamped with a faded seal—a butterfly, wings spread wide.

Clara unrolled it gently. It was a map. Older than the one from the boathouse. Detailed. Marked with annotations in Annie's unmistakable script.

"This is a blueprint," Clara whispered. "Of the inn... and tunnels beneath it."

"There's a passage," Amelia said, tracing a line with her finger. "From the pantry to the old storm cellar—and from there, out to the lake path. That's how Martin was supposed to escape."

"But he never made it," Millie murmured. "Because someone was waiting."

Thunder growled overhead again, closer this time. The wind returned with renewed strength, slamming branches against the roof. But inside the inn, the three women sat motionless, staring at the map that promised both answers and danger.

Lady Grey, her tail curled tightly, let out a low, warning growl.

Whatever truth was buried in the tunnels beneath them, it had waited long enough.

Chapter 18

Secrets Under the Floorboards

The storm outside had raged through the night, the windows of the Tumblebrook Inn reverberating with every clap of thunder. Morning brought little relief. The sky remained iron gray, and the air was thick with the scent of wet pine, damp earth, and something heavier—anticipation. The world outside was muffled, but inside the inn, everything felt heightened: every creak of the floorboards, every whisper of wind beneath the door, every flicker of candlelight. It was as if the building itself were holding its breath, waiting to exhale a truth buried too long.

Amelia Farnsworth stood in the library, the once-comforting scent of leather-bound books now tinged with mildew and age. The blueprint they had discovered the night before was spread across the desk, weighed down with brass bookends and a steaming mug of coffee. She stared at the inked lines, her finger tracing the thin corridor that ran directly beneath the inn's west wing—beneath this very room.

"If these measurements are right," she murmured, "the tunnel should begin... here."

Clara knelt beside the tall bookshelf that had once concealed the hidden compartment. She pressed her palms flat to the old wood floor and ran them along the seams, her breath fogging in the chill that had crept into the room. Lady Grey prowled nearby, amber eyes alert, tail swishing with curiosity. The storm outside seemed to echo their excitement, adding urgency to their search—the thunder like a distant drumbeat spurring them forward.

Amelia crossed the room, knelt beside Clara, and knocked softly on the floorboards. Most rang solid, dense with age. But one thudded with a distinctly hollow resonance.

"There," Clara said, her voice hushed, anticipation trembling in her tone.

They worked quickly, using a fireplace poker and a crowbar from the maintenance closet to pry up the board. Dust billowed as they revealed a recessed wooden hatch sealed with rusted iron latches. The air that rose smelled of time—old, forgotten, heavy with secrets. A breath of history, stale and unwilling to be disturbed.

Lady Grey chirped and batted at the edge of the hatch.

"You really are the brains of this operation," Amelia said, scratching behind the cat's ear.

It took both of them to break the seal. The hinges groaned like a ship straining at its moorings. A stale, damp gust escaped from the opening. A wooden ladder descended into darkness.

Clara clicked on her flashlight and shone it down. "Looks sturdy. Shelves. Boxes. Crates. Looks like no one's been down there in decades."

Amelia grabbed another flashlight and stepped carefully onto the ladder, boots creaking on each rung. At the bottom was a small room, barely six feet high, lined with shelves. Dusty trunks and metal file boxes lined the stone walls. The air was dense with old paper and something else—cedar? Ink? Possibly mold.

Clara followed, her beam sweeping over faded labels and ledgers. "This must be Annie's secret archive. It's more extensive than I imagined."

Amelia opened the nearest box. Inside: pages of notes, meeting logs, correspondence, annotated maps, legal documents. She pulled one and read aloud:

"April 3, 1958. Dispute between M. Hale and R. Harrington regarding felling limits on North Ridge. Hale presented photographic evidence of unauthorized clear-cutting."

Clara found a file labeled Tumblebrook Timber Survey, 1955–1960. Inside were logging permits—some official, others unsigned. "This is everything. Illegal activity. Concealed permits. Bribery. If this ever went public..."

Amelia nodded. "It would shake the very foundation of the town."

Box by box, they cataloged what they could. Annie had recorded everything: Martin Hale's quiet war to preserve Tumblebrook's natural borders, the Harrington family's role in burying his resistance under contracts, disappearances, and smear campaigns.

"Look at this," Clara whispered, pulling out grainy black-and-white photos. Tree stumps ringed with scorch marks. "This wasn't ordinary logging. Aggressive. Fast. No replanting. No permits. And burn marks? That's rushed."

Amelia's stomach turned. "They were stripping the land. And Annie was documenting every step."

More evidence surfaced: receipts, confessions, even a signed affidavit from a forestry inspector tucked into an envelope labeled: To be used only if I disappear.

They uncovered blueprints of logging sites—marked with hazard signs and a coded key hinting at bribes and zoning changes. Clara read aloud a memo to the now-deceased county commissioner requesting increased oversight. Returned with a single scribbled note: Handle it quietly.

Lady Grey stayed at the top of the hatch, ears flat, pupils wide. Suddenly, she bolted from the library.

"What's she after now?" Clara asked.

Amelia climbed back up, heart pounding. The hallway was empty. But Lady Grey stood at the far end near the stairwell, growling low.

"Is someone there?" Amelia called.

Only the wind answered.

Clara emerged. "You felt it too? The air shifted."

They searched the hall, kitchen, back door. Nothing. But back in the library, one of the untouched ledgers now lay open—flipped to a page neither remembered.

"We're not alone," Clara whispered.

Amelia moved to close the hatch. But something glinted near the bookshelf. A rolled scrap of parchment. She unrolled it. A crude sketch of the inn.

"There are symbols," Amelia said, pointing to Xs and arrows—outer walls, crawlspaces, the chimney flue. "This? It's a tunnel under the garden."

Lady Grey leapt onto the desk, pawing a spot marked with a double-circle.

"Escape routes," Clara said.

"Or entrances," Amelia added.

They stilled. Outside, the storm redoubled. But the true storm—the one decades in the making—was rising beneath their feet.

Back in the archive, they uncovered another box: Gazette clippings dated around Martin Hale's protests. A headline stood out:

LOGGER CLAIMS CORRUPTION AT FESTIVAL. TOWN OFFICIALS DENY ALLEGATIONS.

Amelia studied it. Days after his accusation, Hale was dead.

They worked for hours. Notes and documents piled high. When fatigue slowed their hands, Clara gathered key items into a leather satchel.

"We need copies. Bring this to the historian. Maybe even the media."

Amelia nodded, eyes still on the map. "Let's follow this. If there's another exit—or someone's using these tunnels—we need to know."

Lady Grey jumped from the desk, landed beside the satchel, then padded to the bookshelf again. She began clawing at paneling left of the original compartment.

A soft echo.

"Another cavity," Clara said, raising her flashlight.

Together, they pried the panel free. Inside: hand-written letters, bundled in twine. One lay partially open.

Dearest M— You were right. They're lying. I've seen the papers. If they find out I know, I'm not safe. But neither are you. I'll meet you at the garden trail. Bring the ledger. I'll bring the map. —E

"Eliza," Clara whispered. "She was trying to protect him. Maybe both of them."

Their discovery sat heavy between them. No longer whispers or speculation. These were artifacts—tangible, undeniable, and dangerously real.

Amelia paced, rereading the letter. "She knew. She witnessed it. Maybe more."

"And she disappeared," Clara said. "Just like the truth."

Above them, the wind howled louder—echoing what they'd unearthed.

And deep beneath the inn, something waited.

Chapter 19

The Confrontation

The morning after the storm broke clear and sharp, the air cold and bracing as a blade. Golden sunlight spilled over the sodden rooftops of Tumblebrook, refracting off puddles and illuminating the weary inn with a sense of tentative peace. Yet within the Tumblebrook Inn, Clara Henderson felt anything but peaceful.

She stood at the main dining room window, arms crossed tightly over her cardigan, as if to brace against more than just the chill. Behind her, Amelia stirred a fresh pot of coffee, her silence betraying the same restlessness. The air in the room was laden with tension—like static before lightning. The fire in the hearth snapped and hissed, but even its warmth couldn't drive away the urgency pressing in around them.

They had survived the storm. They had unearthed records that could rock the town's foundations. Now, Clara thought, they had to make sure those truths couldn't be buried again. A gnawing sense of responsibility pulsed beneath her ribs, stronger than fear. If they hesitated now, the consequences could ripple far beyond their own lives.

"We can't keep this to ourselves," Clara said finally, breaking the hush. Her voice trembled slightly, but the resolve behind it was steel. "The town deserves to know. They deserve the chance to reckon with it."

Amelia glanced over, lips pursed, worry etched in the lines beneath her eyes. "You think they'll listen? Even after everything we've uncovered, there are still people who want this buried."

"That's why it has to be public," Clara said. "We plan a town meeting. Call it a historical review if we must, a memorial to Martin Hale—anything to get them to show up. We lay it all out. Names, dates, documents. Let them see it with their own eyes."

Amelia poured two mugs of coffee and handed one to Clara. She took a long sip, the warmth grounding her. "Then let's do it. Tonight. Before someone else tries to silence us."

By midmorning, Clara had posted notices at the post office, the café, the grocer's window, and the town square bulletin board. She labeled the event a "Community Historical Gathering" and emphasized refreshments and remembrance. That part wasn't a lie. They were remembering. Honoring. Confronting. Each pinned notice felt like a small act of rebellion, like lighting a candle against the dark. Clara even handed some out personally, meeting neighbors' eyes, watching expressions shift from polite interest to quiet concern. She overheard whispers as she passed: "Did you see this?", "Is this about old man Hale?", and most tellingly, "Do you think the Harringtons will come?"

Back at the inn, the air was electric. Lady Grey watched the preparations with regal detachment, but even her tail twitched with more than usual mischief. Amelia made calls to townsfolk, inviting those likely to listen—and those who whispered about the past in cautious tones. Millie offered to bring cookies and spiced cider. Clara printed and arranged dozens of copies of the most damning evidence.

They set up chairs in a wide semicircle and laid out the documents in tidy rows. Clara took care to underline key connections—land transfers, ledger entries, maps of the woods and inn. Each sheet was a piece of truth long buried beneath silence and fear.

The scent of cinnamon and pine filled the inn. Lamps glowed with soft yellow light against the gray sky, but even their glow couldn't shake the feeling that something—or someone—was waiting in the shadows. Clara felt it with every creak of the floorboards.

By noon, Clara turned her attention to the inn's hallway. Something felt off. The doors were locked, the windows latched, but the floor bore a faint track of dirt, as if someone had trailed in during the night.

"You cleaned the floors yesterday, right?" she asked Amelia.

"Mopped and dried them myself. Why?"

Clara pointed to the faint trail leading toward the back stairwell. "Someone's been inside. Again."

Amelia's expression darkened. "No one signed the guest log. I double-checked this morning."

"Then they weren't a guest."

They followed the trail upstairs to the hallway near the attic. The last door on the left—normally used for storage—was cracked open. Inside, a pile of linens had been disturbed. A dusty attic window was ajar, letting in a morning draft. And in the dust near the window, they saw a partial shoe print—deep, fresh, undeniable.

Lady Grey bounded up the stairs and halted at the window, meowing insistently. Her paw pressed against the sill.

Clara leaned forward and froze. "Amelia. Footprints."

On the sloped shingles outside, barely visible in the morning light, were muddy shoe prints. They led to the dormer roof overlooking the garden. From there, someone could watch the front entrance, the driveway, even the parlor through the second-story window.

"They were watching us," Amelia whispered.

Clara felt her heart thud hard. "Someone who knew about the hidden compartment. Who wanted to see if we found it."

"And probably didn't like that we did."

They sealed the attic window and made their way down, locking every door and checking every entry. Tension twisted in Clara's chest like a knot. Each latch and deadbolt clicked with finality. They weren't just preparing for a meeting now—they were bracing for a confrontation.

"We're not just chasing ghosts anymore," Amelia said. "We're being hunted."

Clara nodded. "Then let them come. Let them hear what we've found. Let them try to deny it."

With quiet determination, they prepared for the most important night of their lives.

Chapter 20

Gathering Allies

Amelia Farnsworth stood in the center of the Tumblebrook Inn's parlor, a place that had once exuded warmth and comfort but now felt heavy with the weight of revelations. The air was thick with the scent of burning wood from the crackling hearth, and the low, steady hum of voices echoed throughout the room. This was no ordinary gathering.

Around her, the familiar faces of Tumblebrook's residents filled the room. Millie Jefferson sat near the fire, hands clasped in her lap, her eyes downcast but attentive. Ezra, the reclusive artist who lived near the old mill, leaned against the far wall, his expression wary yet focused. Mr. Lark, the bookshop owner, thumbed through a sheaf of old documents, his brow furrowed. Even Doris Finch, who usually thrived on spreading town gossip, was uncharacteristically silent, her lips pressed into a tight line.

The parlor was more crowded than Amelia had anticipated. The tension in the room was palpable, a collective unease that clung like smoke. It wasn't just the firelight that flickered—it was the fearful, darting glances exchanged by those who had already seen or heard too much. Outside, the wind howled, battering the windows with icy rain that hissed against the glass. The inn itself seemed to groan beneath the pressure, its beams creaking in protest.

Amelia cleared her throat, suppressing the anxious flutter in her stomach. "Thank you all for coming," she began, her voice steady despite the tension radiating through the room. "We've uncovered some troubling information—facts that could shake the very foundation of this town. And we need your help to bring it to light."

A murmur rippled through the crowd. Ezra straightened, eyes glinting beneath the brim of his worn cap. "What kind of trouble are we talking about, Amelia?"

Clara stepped forward, holding a worn envelope. "The story of Martin Hale wasn't just a tragedy. It was a silenced warning. We have uncovered evidence of illegal land deals, blackmail, and possibly even murder."

Gasps echoed around the room. Doris raised a hand to her mouth, eyes wide. "Murder? Here?"

She passed around documents—photos of burned trees, newspaper clippings, coded maps. The crowd's faces shifted from curiosity to concern, to horror.

"Not just here," Clara said, scanning the room. "But connected to people we all know. People who have shaped this town's history and controlled its narrative."

Amelia met Millie's eyes. The older woman's face was pale. She looked around and nodded slowly. "The Harringtons," she said, voice unsteady.

"Exactly," Amelia replied, jaw tight. "And if we don't act now, they'll bury the truth again—just like they did with Martin Hale."

Then, Millie shared her story: of the Harvest Festival, the hush after Martin's outburst, the men in suits who walked him away.

Silence fell, thick and oppressive. The fire crackled, and shadows danced along the walls. It was as if the house itself was holding its breath, listening.

Then Clara held up the talisman.

"We believe this belonged to Martin. And this," she lifted the sketch of the inn with marked tunnels, "was meant to keep his findings safe. But someone tried very hard to ensure they never saw light."

Clara laid out more documents on the table: diagrams of property lines, handwritten notes from Annie's journal, newspaper clippings—all pointing to a web of deceit spun by the Harringtons and their allies. Millie leaned forward, eyes narrowing.

"This property," she said, tapping a square marked with a faded X, "That's the old boathouse. Royce Harrington used to meet people there after dark."

"That's where we found the initials—E.H.," Amelia murmured. "Edgar Harrington."

"Could he have run operations from there?" Clara asked.

"Or worse," Ezra said darkly. "It's the perfect place to hide something."

Doris shivered. "What if it's where they kept their secrets buried?"

One man stood and left in silence. Lady Grey tracked him with her eyes until he vanished.

Someone muttered, "We always knew the Harringtons were untouchable. This just confirms it."

"There are things in this town that go back generations," someone else said. "We never wanted to remember. But maybe it's time we do."

Amelia swallowed hard. Outside, the storm churned. Lady Grey, perched on the windowsill, watched intently, her amber eyes tracking something unseen.

Suddenly, the door burst open with a thunderous crack. Everyone jumped. Veronica Harrington strode in, eyes cold, lips curled.

Lady Grey growled and retreated from her perch.

"Well, well," she said. "Quite the little gathering."

"We're just having a community meeting," Amelia replied, voice calm.

"Nothing unusual?" Veronica sneered. Her gaze flicked to the documents on the table. "False accusations, perhaps? Against my family?"

"The truth isn't false," Amelia said evenly.

For a moment, Veronica's mask slipped. Her expression twisted. "Be careful, Amelia. You're digging up graves that were meant to stay buried. In Tumblebrook, the dead don't always rest."

She turned on her heel and strode out, the wind slamming the door shut behind her.

Silence returned. Lady Grey moved to Millie's side, pressing against her leg. Millie's hand trembled as she reached down to stroke the cat.

The fire crackled behind them. For a moment, the inn felt like a courtroom, a confessional, and a cathedral all at once.

"It's now or never," Clara whispered. "We can't let them win."

"We won't," Amelia said. Her voice, like the wind outside, was rising.

"We fight back."

After the meeting, as the room emptied and the candlelight waned, Clara and Amelia cleaned in silence. The emotional weight of the evening pressed down like wet wool. Lady Grey remained by the fireplace, tail draped like a banner across the rug.

The last of the cider was poured out, the last paper collected, when the door creaked open one final time.

A man in a wool coat stepped inside, hat pulled low. His boots were muddy, but his stride was sure. He said nothing. He simply handed a folded envelope to Amelia, tipped his hat, and vanished into the night.

Amelia opened it slowly.

Inside, in slanted handwriting:

Midnight. Riverside trail behind the old mill. Come alone. You want answers? I have them.

Clara exhaled slowly. The firelight caught the fear in her eyes.

"Do you think it's a trap?"

Amelia folded the note. "I think it's a beginning.

Chapter 21

The Riverside Meeting

Clara Henderson stood at the edge of the Tumblebrook River, her boots sinking slightly into the damp, muddy bank. The river was swollen from the recent storm, its currents surging with relentless, furious energy that seemed to mirror the tumult in Clara's own mind. Beside her, Amelia Farnsworth adjusted her coat, her green eyes scanning the misty expanse, searching for any sign of the contact they were supposed to meet.

Lady Grey prowled the bank, her sleek grey fur glistening with a fine mist. Her amber eyes flicked nervously, ears twitching at every rustle of wind through the reeds. The cat had been unusually tense since they'd left the inn, her body low to the ground, gaze snapping from shadow to shadow as if she sensed something lurking just out of sight.

The atmosphere was thick with a haunting, heavy stillness—the kind that muffles sound and distorts reality. Each droplet of rain seemed to carry a weight, a whisper of warning as it pattered against the river's churning surface. The fog had thickened, wrapping the woods and riverbank in a shroud of gray, making the world beyond their immediate sight feel intangible, almost nonexistent.

Amelia shivered, pulling her coat tighter. "I don't like this," she murmured, eyes scanning the treeline. "It's too exposed."

"It's the only way," Clara said, her voice low but resolute. "We need to hear what the contact has to say. If they're telling the truth about the logger and the business deals, it could blow everything open."

A shiver ran through Clara—not just from the cold, but from the river's oppressive presence. It churned angrily, slapping at the bank, echoing the pounding of her heart. The wind sliced through the fog, curling around them like a warning. The trees creaked, their gnarled limbs swaying like skeletal arms. A crow cawed from somewhere deep in the woods, its cry fracturing the silence. A branch snapped—sharp, deliberate—and both women flinched.

"Do you see anyone?" Amelia asked, her breath fogging.

Clara shook her head. "No. But they said to meet here."

A rustle came from the woods behind them. Lady Grey's ears pricked, tail twitching as she stared into the shadows. Clara followed the cat's gaze, pulse quickening.

Then, a figure stepped from the trees—cloaked in a heavy, dark coat and a wide-brimmed hat. They moved slowly, deliberately, as though each step was weighed. The face was obscured by the hat's brim and fog, but Clara glimpsed the sharp line of a jaw and glinting, narrowed eyes. Behind him, the fog stirred with the illusion of other shapes in the dark.

The river roared louder, the wind howling like a dirge. The figure paused, assessing them, then stepped closer, boots splashing in the muddy water.

"You're late," the figure said, voice gravelly, edged with warning.

"And you're hiding your face," Amelia countered.

"Can't be too careful," the contact replied, gloved hands slipping into his coat pockets. "You wanted information. I've got it. But it'll cost you."

"We're not paying," Clara said, voice tight. "You said you wanted to make things right. That you had the truth about Martin Hale."

The figure let out a humorless chuckle. "I do. But setting things right doesn't pay the bills."

Amelia stepped forward. "Tell us, or we walk."

He sighed, casting a glance over his shoulder into the trees. "Fine. You want to know why Hale died? He got too close. Too close to something big—something rooted at the top."

"The Harringtons?" Clara asked.

"Not just them." His eyes glittered beneath the brim. "Hale was sniffing around Royce Harrington's logging contracts. But it wasn't just about land. It was what was under it."

"Buried?" Amelia echoed.

"Evidence. Documents. Proof of a larger operation. A network of fake logging companies funneling money through shell accounts. Hale found out. Tried to go public. They silenced him."

"Who's 'they'?" Clara demanded.

Before he could answer, Lady Grey hissed, her fur bristling. The wind screamed through the trees. Shadows shifted. A twig snapped. Then another.

"We need to go," the contact muttered. "They know I'm here."

"Who's watching?" Amelia pressed.

He gripped her arm, eyes wild. "You didn't hear it from me. But it's bigger than one family. You think you know Tumblebrook? You're scratching the surface."

A loud crash echoed. Footsteps neared.

"We need to move," Clara said.

"What about you?" Amelia asked.

"Forget me. But if you want answers—real answers—go back to the one place no one looked. The boathouse."

Then he was gone, swallowed by the fog. Lady Grey yowled.

"Run!" Clara shouted.

They sprinted up the bank, mud clutching at their boots, wind lashing their faces. Footsteps thundered behind them. Branches clawed at their clothes. The river roared, almost speaking.

The boathouse, Clara thought, heart racing. What would they find when they got there?

Chapter 22

Uncharted Connections

Amelia Farnsworth stood in the grand room of the Tumblebrook Inn, her gaze fixed on the darkening horizon. The storm clouds still lingered, heavy and ominous, casting the town in a gray, somber light. The riverside encounter churned in her mind like the swirling waters of the river itself. The contact's cryptic words echoed through her thoughts, interwoven with the chilling sensation of being watched. The town now felt cloaked in shadows, each corner harboring secrets, ready to lunge forth like ghosts seeking release.

Lady Grey, ever perceptive, sat poised by the window, her amber eyes scanning the outside world with the intensity of a sentinel. Her tail flicked steadily, a metronome of tension. Outside, the wind howled, and tree branches scraped against the glass like skeletal fingers. The cat's fur bristled, her eyes darting side to side as if tracking something unseen — a presence lurking just beyond the veil of mist. The inn creaked and groaned under the strain of the storm, each gust of wind sounding like a warning howl from some ancient spirit.

Amelia took a deep breath, steadying herself. If the contact's information was true, the boathouse might hold answers to Martin Hale's death — or to a broader conspiracy entangling the entire town. But another threat loomed. The police chief's growing suspicions were becoming harder to ignore. His sharp gaze dissected every word she and Clara spoke. They were being watched. The inn now felt like a fishbowl — transparent walls through which every action was scrutinized. The weight of surveillance pressed down on Amelia like a physical force.

She crossed the room, heels clicking softly against the wooden floorboards. The air was thick with the scent of old wood, faint traces of morning coffee, and the steady whisper of burning candles. Clara sat at the long table in the center of the room, stacks of letters and notebooks spread before her like the fragmented pieces of a puzzle waiting to be solved. The fire crackled, casting eerie shadows across the walls, turning the room into a cavern of secrets.

"Anything?" Amelia asked, folding her arms.

Clara shook her head, brow furrowed. "Not yet. But Annie's letters — some of them feel... coded. Look at this one."

She handed over a yellowed sheet. The ink was faded but legible, the letters slanted and rushed. "My dearest friend," it read. "The shadows stretch long over the lake these days. But the heart of the matter is buried deeper than any root. I fear the hands that dig will find more than they sought."

"Who is she writing to?" Amelia asked, heart quickening.

"That's just it — there's no name," Clara said. "And the closing line — 'May the keeper of secrets watch over us both.' That's not her usual tone. It's almost reverent."

"Do you think Annie was in love?"

Clara nodded. "Or hiding something for someone she loved."

A tense silence fell. Outside, the wind shrieked and rattled the panes. Lady Grey leapt from the window and padded across the room, brushing against Amelia's leg before bolting toward the back hallway, tail raised like a banner.

"Follow her," Amelia said. "She's onto something."

They trailed Lady Grey down the corridor, her steps silent. The hallway stretched, shadows lengthening with every step. The air turned colder, heavy with dust and old books. At the end stood a rarely used door — the entrance to the storage attic, once a study.

Lady Grey pawed at the door, eyes fixed on the handle. Clara pushed it open; the hinges groaned in protest. Inside, furniture lay shrouded in sheets, their outlines ghostly. The air was musty, tinged with mildew and faded perfume. The light flickered, thick with the weight of untold secrets.

The cat sniffed the floorboards, then froze, her body tense. Her eyes locked on a rectangle in the wall, barely visible beneath the dust.

"A hatch," Amelia whispered, kneeling.

Clara joined her, brushing away the dust. "It's been painted over."

Amelia drew a pocketknife from her cardigan and slid it beneath the edge. With a tug, the hatch popped open. Inside was a narrow compartment filled with yellowed papers and a single, leather-bound logbook.

Clara opened the logbook, her eyes widening. "Church records. And these entries — 'Sunday Rejoice,' 'Silent Reprisal' — match the days around Martin Hale's death."

"Why would the church keep this?"

"Unless they weren't keeping it. They were hiding it."

Lady Grey meowed softly, gaze fixed on the thickening fog outside. Her fur bristled as the wind pressed against the inn like a battering ram.

Clara shivered. "Something doesn't feel right."

Amelia flipped through Annie's letters. "We're not alone. Someone's watching us."

Millie's voice rang from the hallway. "Amelia! Clara! You need to see this."

They rushed to meet her. Lady Grey darted ahead. Millie held a crumpled paper in her trembling hands.

"I found this in the library archives," she said. "A church membership record."

Amelia took the page. One name had been struck through in red: Edith Harrington.

"She was excommunicated?" Clara read aloud.

"No," Millie said. "She was erased."

Amelia's blood chilled. "Why?"

Millie's voice cracked. "Because she knew too much."

Chapter 23

Close Calls and Wary Hearts

Clara Henderson paced the length of the Tumblebrook Inn's lobby, her nerves frayed and raw as the wind howled outside, slashing rain against the windows. The world beyond the glass seemed warped, as if the storm were a physical manifestation of the chaos unraveling in Tumblebrook — a fury that would not abate until every last secret was unearthed. Thunder rolled like a war drum, each reverberation shaking the inn's foundation, as though the building itself were groaning under the weight of the town's sins.

The air was thick with tension, pressing down on Clara like a leaden cloak. Every creak of the floorboards, every moan of the wind felt like a warning — reminders of what they'd uncovered, and what someone was desperate to keep buried. Rain fell in sheets, cascading down the windows and distorting the view into a shifting blur of shadows and light.

Lady Grey watched Clara from the back of the couch, her amber eyes glinting with a gaze that was equal parts unnerving and reassuring. Her tail flicked rhythmically, a metronome of calm amidst the storm. Occasionally, she let out a low, guttural growl, as if sensing something lurking just beyond the walls. Lightning flashed, revealing warped silhouettes that stretched and twisted — trees or something more sinister?

Clara inhaled slowly, trying to focus. Today, she and Amelia had to remain especially vigilant. The air felt charged with something intangible, a hidden force waiting to disrupt everything. The fire in the hearth crackled, casting jagged shadows that danced like ghosts along the walls. Clara followed their movements, half-expecting one to leap free.

Amelia emerged from the kitchen, holding two steaming mugs of tea. She handed one to Clara and sat beside her. The couch creaked under the shared tension. The wind howled, rain battering the windows like desperate fists. The inn felt like a fortress under siege.

"We need to be careful," Amelia said, voice low. "If Millie's right about Edith Harrington's erasure from the records, it means they've been covering their tracks for generations."

"And if they're willing to erase someone's name," Clara said, frowning, "what else would they do? I don't trust the police chief. He's watching us too closely."

"Then we watch back," Amelia replied. "And find the cracks. People who aren't loyal to the Harringtons — or who might be swayed if they see the tides turning."

Clara nodded and sipped her tea. "Let's get to work."

Later that morning, clad in raincoats, they stepped into the storm. Wind whipped their hair, rain lashed their faces, but they pressed on, boots squelching in the mud as they headed toward the town square. The streets were mostly empty, a few figures scurrying past with heads bowed. The flickering lamps cast warped shadows, puddles reflecting a swirling sky that looked as unsettled as the town beneath it.

The Tumblebrook Café glowed like a hearth in the gloom. Inside, Doris Finch arranged pastries behind the counter. Steam fogged the windows. Patrons hunched over mugs, conversations falling silent as

Clara and Amelia entered. The hush was thick, charged with suspicion.

Doris's eyes narrowed. "Afternoon," she said. "Coffee?"

"Please," Amelia said, managing a polite smile. "And if you have any blueberry muffins left..."

"Last two," Doris replied, placing them on a plate and filling mugs. "Busy morning?"

"You could say that," Clara said, nodding toward the café's back corner. Two men spoke in hushed tones — Albert Harrington and Wyatt, one of his aides.

Clara nudged Amelia. "Let's sit closer."

They took a table within earshot. Lady Grey slipped beneath and prowled closer, her amber eyes fixed on the men.

"We can't keep this up," Wyatt was saying. "If this investigation keeps going, it's all going to come out."

"Then it doesn't," Albert growled. "I had the inn searched. Nothing. But if those two women keep digging..."

"What about the contact?" Wyatt asked. "Can we trust them to stay quiet?"

"They don't have a choice," Albert said. "We've got leverage."

Clara's pulse quickened. Were they talking about the riverside contact — or someone else? Before she could wonder further, the café door slammed open. A gust of wind sent napkins flying and rain spattered across the floor.

A man entered, face obscured by a hood, coat dripping. He passed Albert and Wyatt without a glance, disappearing toward the back.

Lady Grey hissed and bolted beneath the counter. Clara froze, eyes locked on the stranger. The wind screamed outside, and the café's tension rose like a held breath. The Harringtons were watching. The storm, the silence — it all pointed to one truth.

They were running out of time.

Chapter 24

Real Faces, Hidden Lies

Amelia Farnsworth stood at the edge of the town square, her gaze sweeping over the gathered crowd beneath a low, gray sky. The air was thick with unease, a tremor running beneath the surface of Tumblebrook's annual autumn fair. Where there should have been laughter and music, the hum of suspicion buzzed instead—muffled whispers, fleeting glances, and smiles that didn't quite reach the eyes.

It was as if the entire town was holding its breath.

Lady Grey slinked around Amelia's legs, her amber eyes sharp with feline focus. Her tail flicked like a metronome, keeping time with the strange tension that clung to the square. Amelia bent down and gently scratched behind the cat's ears.

"You feel it too, don't you?" she murmured.

Lady Grey blinked once, eyes fixed on a knot of townsfolk whispering near the gazebo. Their gazes darted toward the Harringtons, whose presence on the far side of the square seemed to cast a long, invisible shadow. Edgar Harrington spoke quietly with Sheriff Kline, while Albert loomed nearby, his jaw clenched, expression unreadable.

Amelia shivered. It wasn't just that they were watching—it was that they knew something. She could feel it in their eyes, as though the Harringtons were playing a game where everyone else had yet to learn the rules.

"Amelia!" a voice called.

She turned to see Millie Jefferson hurrying toward her, cheeks flushed, her shawl pulled tight against the wind.

"You're needed at the library."

"Now?" Amelia asked, her heart jumping.

Millie's glance flicked to the Harringtons. "Before they notice."

Without another word, Amelia scooped up Lady Grey, the cat warm and still against her chest, and followed Millie down a narrow alley. The scent of damp leaves clung to the air, and wind funneled through the passage like a warning. Behind them, the fair continued, but its laughter sounded brittle, hollow.

The library emerged from the mist like a relic, its stone exterior slick with rain, windows glowing faintly from within. As they reached the steps, Amelia caught whispers on the wind—snippets of rumors, fragments of betrayals. Somewhere nearby, a door slammed, distant but sharp, and the sound echoed down the alley like a shot.

Inside, the library was hushed and shadowed. The scent of paper, ink, and old wood clung to the air. Tall shelves loomed like sentinels, their contents swathed in half-light. Clara sat at a table near the back, nursing a mug of coffee. A stack of brittle letters lay beside her, some opened, others still sealed with cracked wax.

"You made it," Clara said, eyes flicking to the door as they approached.

Amelia set Lady Grey on the table, and the cat immediately nosed through the letters. She batted one toward Clara with deliberate intent. At the same moment, her ears twitched.

"Someone's here," Amelia whispered.

Clara froze, then nodded. "It's been happening all morning. Little sounds. Doors creaking. Like we're not alone."

The library felt charged, like it was waiting for something.

Clara slid a parchment across the table. "These are Annie's coded messages. But they're not letters—they're telegrams."

Amelia stared. The yellowed slips bore the Tumblebrook Post Office seal, their ink faded but legible. The dates aligned with the final weeks before Martin Hale's death.

"Who were they sent to?"

"They're addressed to 'S.R.' but paid for by 'H.S.' Millie recognized the handwriting—Helen Sloane."

"And 'S.R.'?"

Clara's voice dropped. "Samuel Royce. A name no one's mentioned in years—not since the logging dispute."

Amelia's pulse quickened. Royce's name had surfaced in Annie's journal—an agitator in the feud that preceded Martin's death. "So Helen was sending telegrams to Royce. Why?"

"That's the question," Clara said, spreading the pages out. "They're written in Annie's shorthand. But this one—" She pointed to the most recent telegram. "This one's different."

Amelia leaned in. The words danced with implication:

The tree is rotting, but the root is strong. Watch the library at midnight. The keeper will show the way.

"The keeper," Amelia whispered. "Could she have meant herself?"

"Or someone else," Millie said, glancing toward the far aisle where Mrs. Hensley moved quietly among the stacks, spectral in her pale cardigan and silence.

Outside, a shadow passed across the arched window. Clara's eyes darted toward it. A figure stood motionless in the fog, barely more than a silhouette—and then, just as quickly, it was gone.

Lady Grey tensed, fur rising as she leapt down from the table. Her head turned sharply toward the rear of the library.

Then came the sound—soft, but distinct. A door clicking closed.

They stared at one another in silence. The telegrams, the secrets, the hidden watchers—Tumblebrook's long-buried lies weren't done with them yet.

And somewhere, behind the shelves, someone was still listening.

<h1 style="text-align:center">Chapter 25</h1>

<h1 style="text-align:center">Sifting Through Sand</h1>

Clara Henderson sat at the dining room table in the Tumblebrook Inn, her hands wrapped around a steaming cup of coffee as she stared down at the documents spread before her. Each page, each faded photograph, each scribbled note represented a piece of the puzzle—a fractured image of Tumblebrook's tangled history, truth buried beneath layers of secrets and lies. The inn was quieter than usual, as if the entire building were holding its breath, waiting for the next revelation to surface.

Outside, the wind whistled through the eaves, a mournful sound that echoed Clara's growing dread. The storm felt conspiratorial, its howling wind a chorus of silenced voices, a lament for the dead. Each gust seemed to carry whispers—a fragmented plea, a lost confession begging to be heard.

Lady Grey prowled the room with feline precision, her amber eyes glinting as she paused by the window, ears twitching at the faintest sound. Clara couldn't shake the feeling that they were being watched—that every move they made was monitored by unseen eyes. The air hung heavy, thick with secrets long held in the dark wood of the inn. Shadows stretched longer, darkening the room despite the steady light of the lamp.

She picked up a sheet of paper—one of Annie's journal entries transcribed by Millie. The ink blurred and danced across the page, and Clara blinked hard. There was something here—something just out of reach. The smudged ink gave the sense of urgency, as if Annie's pen had raced to outpace fear itself.

"The truth is buried beneath the sand, but the tides always shift," Clara read aloud.

"It means someone wanted to hide it," Amelia said, entering with a tray of sandwiches and a fresh pot of coffee. The aroma warmed the air. "But eventually, all things surface. You can bury the truth, but it always finds a way through. And when it does, it's rarely gentle."

"Do they?" Clara murmured, rubbing her temples. "Every answer uncovers more lies. It's like walking into a labyrinth with no end. What if this is bigger than we can handle? What if we're just two women in a town full of shadows, up against decades of manipulation?"

"That's what they're counting on," Amelia said, her voice firm. "To make us feel powerless. But we're not. Confusion is their tactic. We've come too far to let it work. We're not backing down."

Lady Grey leapt onto the table, tail flicking. She pawed at a photograph, nudging it toward Clara. It was a group photo from the town's centennial celebration—smiling faces, stiff poses. In the corner, nearly hidden by the crowd, stood Edgar Harrington. His eyes, dark and haunted, stared directly into the lens.

"Look at his eyes," Clara whispered. "It's like he knew."

"Knew what?" Amelia leaned closer.

"That someone would look at this photo years later and see through him. It's the look of a man daring someone to uncover his secret."

Lady Grey meowed, eyes fixed on the window. Clara turned. A shadow flitted across the street—fast, furtive. The wind rattled the glass like fingers tapping from the other side. She shivered, pulling her cardigan tighter. The sensation of being watched deepened.

A sudden crash echoed through the inn. Clara and Amelia sprang to their feet. Lady Grey arched her back, hissing toward the hallway. The storm raged, and somewhere in the inn, a door creaked open.

Footsteps echoed—slow, deliberate. Each step a countdown. Clara met Amelia's gaze. Whatever was coming wasn't just a visitor— it was the past, and it had finally come calling.

Thunder cracked like cannon fire. Lightning lit the room in brief, electric flashes. Shadows fused, forming darker shapes. Lady Grey's gaze never wavered from the door.

And the storm, like a judge at the end of trial, screamed its verdict through the walls.

Chapter 26

Time-Linked Betrayal

Amelia Farnsworth stood in the cavernous records room of Tumblebrook's Town Hall, her eyes scanning the rows of dusty files and crumbling ledgers lining the shelves from floor to ceiling. Dim bulbs cast flickering shadows that stretched across the walls, each movement revealing the weight of secrets stored within. The air smelled of aged paper, ink, and the faint tang of mildew—a room frozen in time, its silence a witness to decades of buried sins.

Each document seemed to vibrate with untold stories. The storm outside slammed against the windows, glass trembling under the wind's assault as if it, too, wanted to expose the lies hidden behind these walls.

The atmosphere was oppressive. The shelves loomed like tombstones, each file cabinet a crypt. Amelia's pulse quickened as she moved deeper into the room, floorboards groaning beneath her boots. Lady Grey followed close behind, amber eyes alert, her movements silent and sure.

"It's all here," Millie Jefferson said, her voice a hoarse whisper. She clutched a worn notebook to her chest, staring at the shelves with wide eyes. "Every transaction. Every dispute. Every lie they tried to hide."

Amelia nodded, jaw tight. "Then we're going to find it."

They made their way to the back of the room, where older records were kept. The chill deepened, and the scent of mold mingled with the acrid trace of old ink. Lady Grey halted, fur bristling as she fixed her gaze on a darkened corner. Amelia's heart pounded. Was someone there?

"Look here," Amelia said, opening a file labeled "1959 – Logging Dispute." Inside were handwritten notes, legal agreements, and letters bearing the Harrington crest. The ink had faded, but the names remained: Royce, Sloane, Harrington, Hale. Words etched with such force the ink had bled through the pages—anger made manifest.

"It's from Samuel Royce to Edgar Harrington," Amelia said. "He's threatening to expose them."

Millie paled. "Royce. The logger's confidant—the one who vanished the night of the bonfire."

"Exactly."

They sifted through document after document. Contracts with inexplicable clauses. Receipts made out to unfamiliar names. Letters filled with cryptic warnings. Everything pointed to a deeper conspiracy. The air grew heavier, thick with the stench of decay and old secrets.

"This isn't just about land," Millie murmured, flipping through a ledger. "It's about power. About control over what Tumblebrook becomes."

Amelia frowned. "What do you mean?"

"Look." Millie pointed. "Payments to nonexistent advisors. Hush money. And here—Royce's name again."

Lady Grey growled low, gaze locked on the corner. Amelia stepped toward it, the air colder still. Crates sat in the shadows, one stamped with the Sloane family crest.

She pried open the top. Inside were old papers and a leather-bound book marked with the Sloane emblem. Her hands shook as she opened it.

Meticulous entries filled the pages: "H.S. — protection for Hale property." "E.H. — ensure silence." "S.R. — remove obstacle."

"This is a payoff ledger," Amelia said tightly. "From Helen Sloane."

Millie's voice cracked. "She wasn't protecting the logger. She was protecting herself."

"And Royce," Amelia added. "They were in it together."

The room seemed to contract. Millie clutched her chest. "All this time..."

Amelia closed the book. "We know now. And we're not letting them get away with it."

Lady Grey's eyes stayed locked on the dark corner. The storm outside surged. Amelia felt it—a presence. Watching. Waiting.

The lights flickered. The wind howled. Lady Grey hissed, ears flat, eyes wide.

Then, a door creaked open.

And the past stepped closer.

Chapter 27

Reveal and Pause

Clara Henderson stood by the window of the Tumblebrook Inn's parlor, her gaze fixed on the fog-laden street outside. The storm had subsided, leaving behind a gray, murky stillness that hung over the town like a shroud. Raindrops clung to the glass like tears, blurring the view of Main Street and the few remaining pedestrians hurrying by with collars turned up against the damp chill. The wind still carried a haunting wail, an echo of the storm's fury, and the air was thick with the scent of wet leaves and woodsmoke.

Lady Grey sat beside her, tail flicking in slow, rhythmic swipes, her amber eyes narrowed as if she, too, sensed the unease settling over Tumblebrook. The cat's ears twitched, catching sounds imperceptible to Clara, her eyes locked on something unseen in the swirling fog. The town seemed to hold its breath—each storefront a closed mouth, each window a watching eye.

Inside the parlor, the atmosphere was equally tense. The room was filled with a scattered mix of familiar faces and unexpected visitors—allies and adversaries cloaked in polite smiles and carefully chosen words. Conversations hummed in low tones, punctuated by the occasional forced laugh or the clink of a teacup against a saucer. Every exchange carried an undercurrent of suspicion, a sense of something simmering just beneath the surface, waiting to boil over.

The fireplace crackled softly, casting dancing shadows against the walls, but even the warmth of the flames couldn't dispel the chill that lingered in the air. Overhead, the chandelier swayed slightly, the crystals catching the light and casting fractured prisms that danced along the ceiling like restless spirits. The room felt like a stage set for a performance, each player assuming a role, each word a veiled message waiting to be deciphered.

"You're awfully quiet today," Amelia said, stepping up beside Clara and handing her a steaming cup of tea. The fragrant scent of chamomile and lavender wafted up, a small comfort against the chill. "What's on your mind?"

"I'm just thinking," Clara murmured, her fingers tightening around the cup. "Something doesn't feel right."

"What do you mean?" Amelia's green eyes searched her face, concern creasing her brow. "Do you think it's connected to what Millie heard last night?"

Clara didn't answer immediately. Her gaze drifted back to the street, where a figure in a dark coat lingered near the corner, half-shrouded by mist. Their eyes met—just for a heartbeat—and then the stranger disappeared into the fog, leaving behind a prickle of foreboding.

"There are too many people here who shouldn't be," Clara said, her voice low. "Millie overheard a conversation last night—two guests she didn't recognize. They were talking about Annie's journal. About things they shouldn't know."

Amelia's jaw tightened. "You think they're watching us?"

"I think they're doing more than watching," Clara said, setting her teacup down. "I think they're trying to control what happens next."

Across the room, Lady Grey leapt onto a side table, her gaze fixed on a group of guests near the fireplace. Charles Harrington leaned in close to a woman Clara didn't recognize—a woman with sharp eyes and a calculating smile. Their conversation was hushed, but the intensity of their posture spoke volumes.

Before Clara could respond, the inn's front door creaked open. A gust of cold air swept through the room. Conversations stalled. Standing in the doorway was a man Clara hadn't seen in years—a man with a face etched by secrets and a coat heavy with rain.

"Nathan Hale," Clara whispered.

Amelia's eyes widened. "What is he doing here?"

Nathan stepped inside, shaking off his hat. Water pooled at his feet. As his gaze landed on Clara, a slow, knowing smile curved his lips.

"Clara," he said, voice smooth as ever. "It's been a long time."

The silence tightened around them like a noose. Lady Grey crouched on the table, her fur bristling.

"What brings you to Tumblebrook, Nathan?" Clara asked.

"I could ask you the same," Nathan replied. "I hear you've been unearthing quite the mess."

Amelia stepped forward. Her voice dropped to a dangerous whisper. "You need to leave. Now."

Nathan tilted his head. "Alright," he said softly. "But I'm not done here."

He turned and exited, the wind slamming the door behind him. The room exhaled.

The fire popped. A branch snapped outside. Clara and Amelia stood in the thickening silence, knowing full well that Nathan Hale's arrival had changed everything. And whatever came next would test more than their resolve—it would test the soul of Tumblebrook itself.

Chapter 28

Investigative Revelations

Amelia Farnsworth sat in the Tumblebrook Inn's quiet sitting room, the air heavy with the scent of old books and lingering cedarwood. Outside, the wind whistled through the trees, carrying a chill that slipped through the windowpanes. The room was dim, lit only by a small desk lamp and the flickering glow of the fire in the hearth. On the table before her lay a spread of papers, each one carefully arranged into a timeline of events, connecting the fragments of Annie's notes with their recent discoveries.

Amelia leaned forward, her elbows resting on the table as her eyes scanned the documents. Every date, every name, every cryptic journal entry had been transcribed onto a large sheet of paper—a spiderweb of information with the logger's death at the center. Yet despite her efforts, some pieces refused to fit. Each time she approached a breakthrough, new inconsistencies surfaced.

Lady Grey sat on the armchair beside her, amber eyes narrowed, tail twitching in rhythmic alertness. Occasionally, she'd lift her head to stare toward the hallway, ears pricked, as though sensing something Amelia could not.

The fire crackled, casting shifting shadows across the walls. Lady

Grey's ears twitched again, her gaze locked on the hallway. Amelia frowned.

"What is it, girl?" she asked.

Lady Grey let out a low growl—a sound of warning. Amelia looked to the hallway. Empty. But the air felt colder, heavier.

She turned back to the table and picked up a torn page scrawled with charcoal:

"Seek the stones where the truth lies buried — the rocks that hide, the rocks that whisper."

The phrase sent a shiver through her. Thomasite rocks. Native to the region. Known for their translucent sheen and veined patterns. Stones that held secrets.

"The rocks that whisper," she murmured. "But where?"

A sharp knock interrupted her. The door opened before she could rise. Nathan Hale stepped in, coat dripping, eyes scanning the room.

"Busy, aren't we?" he said, voice smooth, but edged.

Amelia straightened. "Did you not understand you're not welcome here, Nathan?"

He shut the door behind him, posture casual but tense. "You didn't give me a chance to explain."

Lady Grey hissed, retreating to a corner, eyes fixed on him.

Nathan's gaze followed her. "Still guarding the truth, are we, little one?"

Amelia crossed her arms. "If you're here to intimidate me, it won't work."

"Intimidate?" His laugh was dry. "You misunderstand me. I'm concerned. You and Clara—you're digging in places better left undisturbed. Annie's journal? Only half the story. And you don't want the rest."

He stepped closer, lowering his voice. "Some things are better left buried."

"Not the truth," Amelia said, her jaw tight.

His expression darkened. "Suit yourself. But don't say I didn't warn you."

As he moved to the door, he glanced at the table. "You're missing pieces. Important ones."

He left. The door clicked shut. Amelia's hands trembled as she reached for the locket on the table.

Lady Grey jumped down, padding silently toward the hallway. At the threshold, she paused, looking back.

Amelia stood. The floor creaked underfoot. She followed Lady Grey down the hallway, past guest rooms and the stairwell, to the back door leading into the garden. Wind howled outside, trees bending beneath its force. Lady Grey slipped through the open door, fur bristling, heading down the path.

Amelia hesitated. Clouds blotted out the moon, casting the garden in near darkness. Still, she followed. Her breath misted in the cold.

Behind the old, crumbling fountain, Lady Grey stopped, staring at a pile of uneven, mossy stones.

Amelia's breath caught. Thomasite.

She knelt, fingers brushing their slick surfaces. One shifted.

Pulling it free, she revealed a hollow space. Inside: a wax-wrapped bundle of letters tied with a fraying ribbon. She untied it with shaking hands.

Annie's handwriting.

"If you are reading this, then the truth is still hidden. The lies still buried. They will not stop until everything is consumed. Find the ones who saw and heard but never spoke. They are the keepers of the fire, the ones who watched it all burn."

Lady Grey stared at her, tail flicking.

Amelia dug deeper. Her fingers closed around a silver locket engraved A.F. Inside: a sepia photograph of two women arm in arm.

Annie and Royce's wife.

An icy wind swept through the garden. Above, the clouds parted briefly, casting pale moonlight over a shadow slipping behind the fence.

"Amelia!" Clara's voice rang from the inn. "You need to come back inside. Now."

Amelia rose, clutching the locket and letters. Lady Grey stayed near the stones, staring into the darkness.

Inside, the warmth felt foreign. Clara stood by the fire, face pale.

"What is it?" Amelia asked.

Clara handed her a crumpled note. "It was shoved under the door."

Amelia unfolded it. Scrawled in harsh strokes:

"You're digging in the wrong places. Keep going, and you'll end up just like her."

The locket in her hand felt heavier than ever, as if echoing a heartbeat from the past.

Chapter 29

Encounters with Key Players

Clara Henderson sat in the bookshop's back room, surrounded by stacks of aging records and crinkled newspapers. The scent of ink and paper was thick in the air, mingling with the faint aroma of tea steeping in the corner. Outside, the sky had darkened to a heavy slate gray, rain pattering against the windows in a relentless rhythm. It was as though the entire town of Tumblebrook was being washed clean, the storm pressing down with an insistent, unyielding force. The wind howled through the narrow alleyways, rattling the glass panes and making the old wooden beams groan with the weight of buried secrets.

The trees swayed violently, their branches clawing at the sky as if trying to escape the oppressive gloom. Each gust sent a chill through the room, and Clara shivered despite the warmth of the tea clasped between her hands. Her eyes moved over the stacks of records, each one a puzzle piece, a fragment of the past waiting to be assembled into a cohesive, damning picture.

As she sat there, the room seemed to shrink, the shadows deepening with every roll of thunder. It was as though the storm carried the weight of every whispered confession that had gone unheard.

Clara leaned forward, fingers tapping thoughtfully against a thick ledger bound in cracked leather. The title was faint, almost illegible, but she could just make out the words: "Tumblebrook Accounts and Holdings - 1959." A shiver ran down her spine. This was the year Annie had pinpointed as the fulcrum of everything — the logger's death, the land disputes, the fire.

Millie had called Clara earlier, her voice trembling, hinting at new connections between key players in the town's history. Connections that could upend everything they thought they knew. Clara couldn't shake the image of Millie's wide, fearful eyes. The words Millie had whispered echoed in Clara's mind: "They're watching us, Clara. They know."

Clara flipped open the ledger, scanning lists of transactions, property transfers, and acquisitions. Names leaped off the page — Harrington, Hale, Royce. Beside her, Lady Grey perched on a stack of books, her ears twitching at the faintest sound. Her tail flicked in a slow, steady rhythm, like a metronome counting down to revelation.

"What are we missing, girl?" Clara murmured, running a finger over a smudged entry. "What don't we see?"

Lady Grey's eyes snapped open. She leapt from the books to a far corner of the room, nose pressed to the baseboard. Clara crossed to her, kneeling. She ran her fingers along the wall. One section gave slightly.

With effort, Clara slid the baseboard back, revealing a narrow cavity. Inside was a small wooden box, carved with intricate swirling patterns. Her breath caught. Lady Grey's tail lashed as if affirming the find.

Clara placed the box on the desk and opened the lid. Inside were yellowed photographs from the 1959 Harvest Festival. In one, Royce Harrington stood at the forefront, his hand on the shoulder of an unknown man. In another, a young woman with dark, wavy hair held a bouquet of lilies — the same woman from a photo Clara had found in the boathouse.

At the bottom of the box was a folded note:

"Meet me by the boathouse. Midnight. I have proof."

Proof of what?

Before Clara could speculate further, the shop's bell jingled. She stuffed the photos and note back into the box and turned just as Millie rushed in, flushed and breathless.

"Clara, you need to come quickly," she said. "Amelia just found something — something big."

Clara clutched the box to her chest and followed Millie into the storm. Lady Grey trotted behind, ears pricked. As they ran, Clara couldn't shake the feeling they were being watched.

Inside the inn, the air was charged, thick with tension. Amelia stood in the parlor, ashen and wide-eyed, holding a rusted metal tin. Its lid hung open, revealing yellowed papers.

Clara froze. The tin was identical to the one she'd found.

"What is it?" Clara asked.

Amelia held up a tattered letter. "Proof," she whispered. "Annie wasn't just investigating the logger's death. She was trying to expose an entire network of corruption. And the boathouse was her drop point."

Clara's heart pounded. Lady Grey padded closer, eyes fixed on the tin as though it held every secret Tumblebrook had buried.

Millie's voice trembled. "Oh my God."

Chapter 30

Aligning Forces

Amelia Farnsworth stood in the center of the Tumblebrook Inn's parlor, the room filled with the scent of freshly brewed coffee and the soft rustle of pages being turned. Outside, the rain had lessened to a steady drizzle, a mist hanging over the town like a veil. The fire crackled softly in the hearth, casting long, wavering shadows against the walls. Millie, Clara, and a handful of trusted allies were seated around the room, their expressions a mix of resolve and exhaustion. The dim lighting cast deep shadows, creating an almost conspiratorial atmosphere that underscored the gravity of their gathering.

Lady Grey perched regally on the arm of Amelia's chair, her amber eyes fixed intently on the group. The cat's tail swayed slowly back and forth, a metronome of tension that seemed to echo the collective apprehension in the room. The air was thick with the weight of what they now knew — a decade-spanning conspiracy that had entangled some of the most powerful families in Tumblebrook, all tied to Martin's death and the subsequent cover-up.

Amelia took a deep breath, the air cool in her lungs. She glanced around the room, eyes settling on each face present. Ezra, the eccentric artist, sat hunched forward, his thick brows drawn tight as he stared at the fireplace, his mind clearly racing with recollections of the past. Eleanor Vance, the town's librarian, clutched a thick binder to her chest, her eyes darting nervously around the room as though expecting a shadow to lurch forward from the corners. Millie sat closest to Amelia, her hands wringing in her lap, her lips pressed into a thin, worried line.

"We can't afford to make any more missteps," Amelia said, her voice steady but low. "Every move we make from here on has to be calculated, precise. We're not just dealing with a murder cover-up. We're dealing with a system of control that's been in place for decades."

Eleanor swallowed audibly, her knuckles white against the dark binder. "I found these," she said, sliding the binder across the table toward Clara. "Records of property transfers from 1958 through 1961. There's a pattern — a very deliberate one."

Clara opened the binder, her eyes narrowing as she scanned the pages. "Royce Harrington," she muttered, tracing her finger down a column of names. "Edgar Hale. Martin Royce. Every name on this list is connected to Martin Hale in some way."

"What kind of pattern?" Millie asked, leaning forward.

"Each property that changed hands coincides with a major event — a fire, a disappearance, an accident," Clara said, flipping through the pages. "It's as if Royce was using tragedy as a cover to seize control of assets."

"That's exactly what he was doing," Amelia said, her jaw tightening. "Royce wasn't just consolidating land. He was consolidating power."

Millie leaned forward, her fingers wrapped around a steaming mug of tea. "But how can we be sure we're not being watched? If they know we're onto them—"

"They already know," Clara interjected, her eyes sharp as she glanced at the stack of papers spread across the coffee table. "That's why they're escalating. The anonymous threats, the break-ins, the shadowy figures. They're trying to intimidate us into silence."

Amelia nodded, the lines around her mouth tightening. "And that's why we need to regroup. We've been reactive, responding to each threat as it comes. But now, we take control. We take the fight to them."

Lady Grey leapt gracefully to the floor, padding over to a stack of files Clara had been reviewing. The cat nudged the top folder with her nose, flipping it open to reveal a map of the logging sites surrounding the lake — each marked with red ink, representing a piece of land acquired by Royce Harrington over the last three decades.

"These acquisitions weren't random," Clara said, her voice hard. "Royce was building something — a network. And every property connects to another, forming a web that ties back to Martin's death."

Millie frowned, leaning closer to study the map. "But what was he after?"

"Control," Amelia said, her jaw set. "And if we're going to bring that control to an end, we need to expose every link in that web."

The fire crackled louder, sending a cascade of embers into the hearth. Outside, the rain continued to fall, each drop a steady, rhythmic beat against the glass — a countdown to the storm that was still to come.

Ezra cleared his throat, his voice gravelly and hesitant. "I remember seeing Royce and Edgar Hale together right before the fire. They were arguing in the alley behind the café. Edgar was shouting something about debts and threats — said Royce was taking things too far."

"Debts?" Clara asked, her brow furrowing. "What kind of debts?"

"Money," Ezra said, his eyes darkening. "But not just money. Secrets. Edgar knew something about Royce — something big. That's why he was silenced."

Amelia exchanged a glance with Clara, her heart pounding. "We need to find out what Edgar knew. If it's in Annie's notes, we have to cross-reference everything."

Later that night, the rain had subsided, leaving the air heavy and damp, the mist rolling off the lake like a living, breathing entity. Amelia and Clara stood at the edge of the boathouse, their flashlights casting narrow beams of light that cut through the murky darkness. The old wooden structure creaked with each gust of wind, the scent of wet wood and algae rising from the water.

"Are you sure about this?" Clara whispered, her eyes darting around nervously.

"We need to know what Annie left behind," Amelia said, her jaw tight. "If she was using the boathouse as a drop point, there has to be more."

They stepped inside, the floorboards groaning beneath their weight. Shadows loomed large, the outline of the rowboat swaying gently against the dock. Lady Grey slinked in behind them, her eyes gleaming like twin lanterns in the darkness.

Amelia moved toward the far wall, her flashlight beam tracing over the worn wooden planks. "Look here," she said, pointing to a section of the wall where the boards didn't quite align. "It's been pried open before."

Clara knelt down, her fingers tracing the gap. "There's something wedged inside."

Before they could pry the board loose, a sudden creak echoed from behind them. Both women turned sharply, their flashlights slicing through the dark to reveal a tall, shadowed figure standing at the boathouse entrance.

"Looking for this?" the man said, stepping forward into the pale beam of Clara's flashlight. He was older, with graying hair and a weathered face, his eyes sharp and calculating. In his gloved hand, he held a small, metal box — identical to the one they had found in the wall at the inn.

"Who are you?" Amelia demanded, her fists clenched.

"Name's Jacob Hale," the man said, his voice low and gravelly. "And I have what you're looking for."

Clara's breath caught in her throat. "Hale? As in—"

"Yes," Jacob said, his jaw tightening. "As in the brother of Martin — the one they tried to silence."

Amelia and Clara exchanged a glance, shock and disbelief coursing through them.

Jacob stepped closer, holding out the box. "Inside here — everything Annie uncovered. Names, dates, payments. It's all here. But it's not safe to talk here. I'll come to you."

Before they could respond, Jacob stepped back into the shadows, his footsteps fading into the night. The wind carried the faint echo of his final words:

"Time's running out."

Chapter 31

Web of Lies

The storm had finally passed, but Tumblebrook remained steeped in a heavy, oppressive silence. The streets were empty, the sky a slate gray, and the air hung thick with the scent of wet earth and lingering tension. Puddles pooled in the dips and hollows of the uneven road, reflecting the bleak, cloud-choked sky like shards of a broken mirror. A few leaves skittered across the pavement, tumbling end over end as the wind moaned through the trees, carrying the ghostly whispers of the town's buried secrets. The entire town seemed to hold its breath, waiting for the next strike—the next revelation that could shatter its fragile calm. Windows remained shut tight, doors bolted, as if the very walls were afraid to let the darkness in.

Inside the inn, Amelia stood at the window, her gaze fixed on the road that wound its way through town, her mind churning through the events of the past few days like a relentless tide. Every word, every threat, every warning echoed in her head, building to a deafening crescendo. Her hands trembled at her sides. She forced herself to take a deep breath, releasing it slowly. There was no room for fear now. Only action—the desperate, urgent need to make sense of the chaos that had engulfed their lives. A sense of impending doom pressed down upon her like a weight.

Lady Grey sat perched on the windowsill, her amber eyes fixed on the street below. Her tail flicked back and forth, fur bristling as though she could sense the unseen forces still lingering, like phantoms haunting the town. The inn felt colder, emptier, as if the walls themselves had absorbed the fear and uncertainty permeating every corner of Tumblebrook. Shadows deepened, corners darkened, secrets pressing close to the surface.

Clara paced the length of the common room, arms crossed tightly, brow furrowed in deep concentration. On the table lay a chaotic sprawl of notes, newspaper clippings, and photographs, connected by red string that crisscrossed the surface like a spiderweb of deceit. Annie's journal lay open, pages marked with Clara's frantic scrawls. The words leapt out like accusations—reminders of uncovered secrets and dangers still ahead.

"We're missing something," Clara said, voice tight, eyes darting over the papers. "We're so close—I can feel it. But there's something we're not seeing. Something right in front of us."

Amelia turned from the window, jaw clenched. "Too many pieces. Not enough connections."

"Maybe that's the point," Millie offered from the armchair near the hearth, hands wrapped around a mug of tea. "Maybe they made it confusing on purpose. Kept things scattered, disjointed."

"Exactly," Clara muttered, eyes narrowing on a newspaper clipping. "Deliberately misleading."

"What do you mean?" Amelia asked, moving beside her.

"Think about it," Clara said, finger trailing a line of red string from Martin's death to the disappearance of Jacob's brother. "Every lead—every step—it's been misdirection. What if that's how they kept us chasing our tails?"

"You think there's a larger connection?" Amelia asked.

Clara nodded. "Martin's death. Jacob's brother. Annie's threats. They all lead back to the same people. But we didn't see it. Until now."

"What changed?" Millie asked, leaning forward.

"This." Clara held up a torn piece of paper—the letter found beneath the floorboards. The handwriting was shaky, the ink smudged, but legible:

I know what you did. You can't hide it forever.

"It was addressed to Annie," Clara said, her voice hard. "But never sent. She was going to confront them."

"Confront who?" Amelia asked.

"The board," Clara whispered. "The same people who hired the Fixer. The ones who wanted Annie gone."

"The Fixer?" Millie voice showing their shared concern.

"The man who fixes all the Board's problems, making people disappear..."

A chill ran through Amelia. "You think they're still watching us?"

"I think they never stopped," Clara said. "They've been here all along."

Lady Grey hissed, ears flattened, eyes locked on the window. Amelia followed her gaze.

Across the street, a dark figure stood beneath the awning of the old general store. His face was obscured by the brim of his hat. His posture was rigid, shoulders squared—as if daring them to acknowledge him.

"Who is that?" Millie whispered.

"I don't know," Amelia said, fists clenching. "But I intend to find out."

She moved toward the door, pulse racing. Lady Grey leapt from the sill, body tense, gaze fixed on the figure outside. The wind howled as Amelia stepped into the cold, the air biting at her skin.

The figure didn't move.

From the corner of her eye, Clara saw another silhouette under a streetlamp—same posture, same stillness.

"They're multiplying," Clara breathed. "They're not just watching us. They're closing in."

The wind picked up. A wolf howled in the distance.

Lady Grey's fur bristled. Her eyes remained fixed on the darkness ahead.

Chapter 32

Truths Uncovered

The rain drummed against the windows of Tumblebrook Inn like a thousand tiny fists, a relentless, driving force that mirrored the tension mounting within its walls. Each drop struck like a warning, a sinister cadence that echoed the pounding of Amelia's heart. Inside, the fire crackled in the hearth, but its warmth did little to dispel the chill that had settled deep into her bones. The storm outside was nothing compared to the tempest in her mind—a relentless churn of thoughts, each more disturbing than the last. The inn creaked and groaned, amplifying her unease, as though the house itself were breathing, listening, waiting.

Clara sat cross-legged on the floor, her back against the sofa, surrounded by a semicircle of crumpled papers, photographs, and hastily scribbled notes. Each piece was a fragment of the puzzle they'd been assembling for months, shards of a darker truth now taking shape. The flickering fire cast shifting shadows across the walls, as if the room were alive and aware, watching them dig up the past. Every time Clara reached for a new piece of evidence, her hands trembled slightly, her breath shallow with the weight of what they were uncovering.

Lady Grey prowled the perimeter of the room, amber eyes glinting in the firelight. Her ears twitched at sounds too faint for human hearing, her tail flicking with agitation. She stopped often to glare at the windows, fur bristling, as if the very air carried the scent of danger. The room thrummed with tension, every creak of the floor, every flicker of flame, adding to the sense of an unseen presence pressing close.

"What are we missing?" Clara muttered, frowning at the papers. "We have the letter Annie wrote, the clippings, the ledger entries, the list of properties Nathaniel bought under aliases. Everything connects to Martin's death, but we can't pinpoint the final link. We're drowning in evidence, but still short of the truth."

"We're not missing anything," Amelia said, jaw tight, eyes on the rain-blurred street outside. "We just haven't arranged it the right way yet."

"What about Nathaniel?" Millie asked softly, wringing her hands near the table. "He's been at the center of this since the start."

Nathaniel Hale. His name carried weight in Tumblebrook. Once respected, connected, powerful—then corrupted. Over time, he'd aligned with those who operated in the shadows. He was Jacob's older brother—the one who used to look out for them, the one who vanished when the town needed him most.

"Nathaniel wasn't always like this," Jacob had said once, voice hollow. "He used to be... good."

But that was before Martin's death. Before the Fixer. Before Nathaniel became a ghost—present in whispers, but never seen.

"He knew what happened to Martin," Clara said, jaw clenched. "He was there."

"But he never said a word," Amelia added darkly. "Not to Annie. Not to Jacob. Not to anyone."

"Because he was protecting himself," Clara said bitterly. "Or someone else."

"The Fixer," Millie whispered. "Or worse."

A sharp knock broke the air. All three women flinched. Lady Grey bolted behind the sofa, eyes wide.

"Who could that be?" Millie asked, pale.

"Stay here," Amelia said, rising. The fire cast long shadows as she crossed the room. Each step was heavy, the air thick with dread. She opened the door a crack. "Who is it?"

"It's me," Jacob said, soaked from the rain, eyes wide. "Let me in."

Amelia stepped back. Jacob staggered inside, drenched and shaking.

"You look like hell," Clara said. "What happened?"

"Nathaniel," Jacob said, pacing like a caged animal. "He's gone."

"Gone?" Amelia's heart lurched. "What do you mean?"

"I went to confront him. His place was trashed—furniture overturned, papers everywhere. Someone got to him first."

"Was there blood?" Clara asked.

"No. But I found this." He handed Amelia a crumpled paper.

Amelia unfolded it, eyes scanning the hastily written message: "You know too much. You talk, you die."

"It's the Fixer," Jacob growled. "Tying up loose ends."

"Or silencing anyone who could expose him," Clara said.

"We need to move," Amelia said, tossing the note aside. "If Nathaniel's gone, we're next."

"But where?" Millie asked, panicked. "If they got to him, they're watching us."

Amelia looked toward the window—and froze. Outside, beneath the awning of the old general store, a dark figure stood watching, his face hidden by the brim of his hat. Another stood farther back, barely visible in the alley shadows.

"They're already here," she whispered. "We're out of time."

Chapter 33

The Ties That Bind

The rain had finally subsided, but the air remained heavy, dense with the scent of wet earth and rotting leaves. The inn's common room was dimly lit, the fire in the hearth a mere flicker of its former self. Shadows danced along the walls, twisting and contorting as if they carried the secrets the room had absorbed over the years. The silence hung like a thick fog, pressing down on everything, suffocating and inescapable.

Amelia sat at the dining table, her hands clasped around a cup of lukewarm tea. She hadn't taken a sip in over an hour. Her mind churned with every word Jacob had said, every implication of Nathaniel's disappearance, and every dark shadow now looming over Tumblebrook. It felt as though the entire town had been swallowed by a darkness that refused to lift.

"What if they already have him?" Millie asked, her voice tremulous as she leaned against the wall, arms crossed protectively over her chest. Her usually warm eyes were now haunted, rimmed with dark circles that spoke of sleepless nights. "What if they're doing to him what they did to Annie?"

The words hung heavy in the room, a grim reminder of what had happened to Annie Farnsworth — a fate shrouded in mystery and silence.

"We don't know that," Clara said, pacing the length of the room. The floorboards creaked beneath her steps, the sound echoing through the hush. "We don't know anything yet. But we do know this — Nathaniel knew more than he let on. And now he's gone."

"Nathaniel wasn't always like that," Jacob said, his voice strained as he lifted his head. "There was a time he would've done anything for us. For me. For Tumblebrook. But then... then he met the Fixer. And everything changed."

"The Fixer," Clara echoed, her jaw tightening. "The man who promised power and delivered poison."

"Nathaniel wasn't just a businessman," Millie added, glancing at Jacob. "He was a confidant to many of the town's most powerful. He knew things — things people would kill to keep secret."

Jacob swallowed. "He was my brother. But near the end, I barely recognized him. He'd go days without speaking to me. Lock himself in his office, make calls, scribble in that damn notebook. He always said he was protecting me. But I think... he was protecting himself."

Lady Grey prowled along the windowsill, eyes fixed on the street outside. Her tail swished in slow, deliberate arcs. Though the street was empty and cloaked in fog, the tension remained — as if the town itself held its breath. The mist pressed against the glass like a living thing, watchful and still.

"We need to regroup," Amelia said, her voice steadier than she felt. "Let's go over what we know — what we suspect, and what's still missing."

Clara stopped pacing and moved to the table. "Let's start from the beginning."

Amelia took a breath and laid the crumpled note Jacob had brought onto the table, smoothing it with her palm. The ink was still faintly damp, the words smeared but legible:

"You know too much. You talk, you die."

"It's the Fixer's work," Clara said, her eyes narrowing. "Nathaniel wasn't just caught up in this. He was working for them."

"But why?" Millie whispered. "Why would Nathaniel do that? He was one of us. He was Jacob's brother."

"Maybe that's exactly why," Jacob said bitterly. "Because he knew no one would suspect him."

"He wasn't always like that," Clara murmured. "He cared once. About Tumblebrook. About us."

"That was before the Fixer," Jacob said. "Before the deals. Before the lies."

"Hiding bodies?" Millie repeated, eyes wide. "Are you saying he was involved in... murder?"

Jacob didn't answer immediately. "I'm saying Nathaniel wasn't just a pawn. He was a player. And he knew exactly how to move the pieces."

A heavy silence followed. Outside, the fog grew denser, the windows now mere veils to the outside world. The fire's glow dimmed further, and the room seemed to shrink, the air closing in.

"If he was a player," Amelia said, staring down at the note, "he wasn't acting alone. There are others."

"Others who know what happened to Martin," Clara added. "Others who know why Annie was silenced. And who the Fixer really is."

"And now they're coming for us," Jacob said. "Because we know too much."

Lady Grey let out a low growl, her gaze locked on the window. Outside, a shadow moved — a dark silhouette slipping through the mist.

"We need to find Nathaniel," Amelia said, rising. "If he's alive, he knows everything."

"And if he's not?" Clara asked, her voice taut.

Amelia met her gaze. "Then we find the Fixer. And we end this — once and for all."

Chapter 34

Webs of Deception

The wind howled through the trees surrounding Tumblebrook, branches swaying like ghostly fingers clawing at the night sky. Inside the inn, the atmosphere was just as tense, each room heavy with foreboding. The air was thick with the weight of everything left unsaid, every secret still hidden. Shadows clung to every corner, deepening the darkness that seemed to have taken root in Tumblebrook. The wind's relentless howl grew louder—a haunting wail that sounded almost human, as if the storm itself were crying out in warning. The night had wrapped the town in a suffocating grip, making every creak, every groan of the old inn feel like a ghostly murmur.

Amelia stood at the window, eyes narrowed as she scanned the street below, fingers drumming anxiously against the glass. The rhythmic tap echoed through the room—a steady beat against the silence. The rain had stopped, but the mist lingered, hanging low and thick, distorting familiar shapes and turning known streets eerie. Every shadow seemed to shift and pulse, as if alive with secrets, the town holding its breath in anticipation. The fog pressed in from all sides, making the inn feel like an island adrift in a sea of uncertainty.

Behind her, Clara and Millie sat at the dining table, a pile of documents, photographs, and hastily scrawled notes spread before them like the fractured pieces of a shattered mirror. Lady Grey lay curled atop the table, her tail flicking as her eyes followed every movement. Her ears twitched at each sound—the creak of a floorboard, the distant howl of wind, the faint murmur of voices that may have been real or merely echoes of fear. Her sharp amber eyes glinted in the dim light, her muscles taut as though bracing for something—or someone—to strike.

"We're running out of time," Clara muttered, brow furrowed as she leaned closer to the documents. "The more we dig, the more it feels like we're only scratching the surface. Nathaniel, the Fixer, Martin's death—they're all connected, but the links are buried under layers of lies. The more we pull, the more tangled it gets."

"We need to focus," Amelia said, still watching the foggy street. "Was Nathaniel forced into working with the Fixer? Or was he playing both sides—protecting himself while covering up the logger's death? Or worse, was he orchestrating all of it, manipulating everyone while pretending to be a victim?"

Millie bit her lip, twisting a fraying handkerchief in her lap. "What if it's more than that? What if he was protecting someone? Someone we haven't considered—someone close."

Clara looked up sharply. "Someone else? Who?"

"Think about it," Millie whispered. "Nathaniel was untouchable—until recently. What if someone close to him was being used against him? What if he was blackmailed into silence? Or hiding someone's sins to protect them?"

"Like Jacob," Amelia said quietly. "Or Annie. Or someone from Nathaniel's past. Someone who still has a hold on him."

The room fell silent. Outside, the wind lashed against the windows, glass rattling like a warning. Lady Grey sat up, ears pricked, eyes fixed on the door. The tension pressed down, making every breath feel labored. The silence grew heavy, the room itself seeming to hold its breath.

"Nathaniel knew something about Annie's death," Clara said, standing. "It's time we found out what."

"How?" Millie asked. "If he's gone, how do we get answers?"

"We go back to where it all started," Clara said. "The boathouse."

Amelia's jaw clenched. That place had always felt like a haunting ground for the past—heavy with secrets, the air thick with rot and memory. The ground itself whispered of things long buried.

"If Nathaniel left anything behind, it'll be there," Amelia said. "And if the Fixer's watching us, he'll be watching there, too."

Millie's gaze darted to the window, where shadows danced just beyond the glass. "Then we'd better be ready."

Clara nodded. "We're walking into a web of deception. And this time, we might not come out alive."

"We need to be smart," Amelia said firmly. "No more walking in blind. We need to anticipate every trap, every betrayal. Think like Nathaniel. What would he have done if he knew someone was closing in?"

Lady Grey growled low, her gaze locked on the door. Outside, the wind rose again, branches slapping the windows, shadows stretching like clawed fingers across the walls. The fire flickered, the room trembling with tension.

"What if we're already being watched?" Clara asked, glancing at the windows. "What if they're expecting us?"

Amelia's eyes hardened. "Then we make sure they don't know when. We keep them guessing."

"We need to move in silence," Millie said. "Without being seen."

"Easier said than done," Clara muttered. "But we have to try."

"Because if we don't," Amelia said, voice low and resolute, "we might not get another chance."

Chapter 35

The Reckoning

The wind lashed against the windows of Tumblebrook Inn, rattling the glass with an urgency that echoed the turmoil inside. The common room was cloaked in darkness, save for the dim glow of the fire, its flames licking hungrily at the air and casting restless shadows that pulsed and breathed against the walls. The room felt smaller, the ceiling lower, as if the very inn itself was holding its breath, waiting for the inevitable clash that loomed on the horizon. The wind howled with an eerie intensity — a mournful, wailing sound that echoed the town's collective fear. Outside, the storm raged, rain pouring in sheets against the roof, the gusts like a chorus of voices crying in despair.

The world beyond the window was a swirling void of fog and darkness. Trees swayed violently, their branches clawing at the sky like desperate fingers. Every few moments, a flash of lightning illuminated the street, casting stark glimpses of the mist-shrouded town. Tumblebrook was steeped in shadow, every house dark, every alleyway a yawning pit of black.

Inside, the tension was suffocating. The walls seemed to lean inward, bracing against some unseen force. The scent of burning wood hung in the thick air. The fire crackled and hissed, flames flickering erratically as if caught in a battle against the dark. Every pop sounded like a warning, every sizzle like a whisper.

Amelia stood at the window, her fingers tight on the frame. The fog was so dense it rendered the world beyond the porch invisible. It was as though the inn were an island in a void, stranded and isolated. The wind howled like a beast, its wail sending a shiver through her spine. Each gust felt like a warning.

"They're watching us," Clara said, her voice taut as she paced, fists clenched. Her eyes flicked between the window and the front door, braced for an ambush. "I can feel it. They know we're closing in. They're just waiting to strike."

"They already have," Jacob said from the mantle, his voice leaden. He stared into the fire, its flames dancing like they whispered secrets. "Nathaniel's gone. Martin's death is still unsolved. And the Fixer? He's tightening the noose."

Millie perched on the couch's edge, wringing her handkerchief. "What if they come for us next? What if they decide we know too much?" Her voice was hushed, as if the walls were listening.

"We're not letting that happen," Amelia said, yanking back the curtain a sliver to scan the street. The fog pressed against the glass like a living thing. "We stay smart. Focused. We have to think like them."

"Think like them?" Clara stopped pacing, brow furrowed. "You mean become them."

"No," Amelia said, turning from the window. "We anticipate. The Fixer is playing chess — we've been pawns. But we can turn the game. Make them think we're weaker or know more than we do."

"How?" Jacob asked, pushing off the mantle. "Nathaniel's gone. And the Fixer? He's a ghost."

"Maybe not a dead end," Amelia said, her resolve sharpening. "Nathaniel met someone at the boathouse. Someone who knew the Fixer. Maybe he left something behind."

"A ghost with real allies," Clara said, grabbing a paper from the table. "We need to go over it all again — Martin's records, Nathaniel's meetings, Annie's notes. We missed something."

Lady Grey leapt onto the table, eyes fixed on the document in Clara's hand. She let out a low growl, ears flat, tail lashing. Her gaze shifted to the door.

"She's right," Millie said. "It's all connected — Annie, Martin, Nathaniel. But how?"

"Maybe it's not what we're missing," Amelia said, stepping closer to Clara. "Maybe it's what we're not seeing. What they've hidden."

"What do you mean?" Jacob asked.

Amelia pointed at Annie's notes. "Here — she mentions Martin arguing with someone at the boathouse, but she never names him."

"Maybe she didn't know," Millie said. "Or maybe she couldn't say."

"She left clues," Clara said, scanning the page. "A trail."

"Breadcrumbs leading to the Fixer," Amelia said, eyes fierce. "We need to know who was at that boathouse. Now."

"But how?" Jacob asked. "Nathaniel's gone. We don't know who he met."

"Unless..." Clara locked eyes with Amelia. "Unless he left something."

Jacob and Clara exchanged a glance. Millie twisted her hands.

"What if we're being watched?" Millie asked.

"Then we make sure we're not seen," Amelia said, grabbing her coat. "We go now."

Minutes later, they slipped through the back door into the storm. Rain drenched them instantly. The path to the boathouse was slick with mud, each step dangerous. The fog cloaked everything, muffling the world.

The boathouse loomed like a phantom, its windows dark. Lightning flashed, briefly revealing its warped frame. Wind howled through its boards.

Inside, the scent of mildew filled the air. Floorboards groaned beneath their feet. Clara's flashlight swept the room.

"Here," she whispered, crouching.

A leather notebook lay on the floor. Its pages were damp but readable.

"It's Nathaniel's," Amelia said, breathless. "Meetings, names, times. He was tracking the Fixer."

"He knew more than he said," Clara whispered.

Before Amelia could reply, a crash rang out. The door burst open. Rain and wind surged in. In a flash of lightning, a shadow filled the doorway.

"Run!" Jacob shouted.

The storm screamed — and the darkness swallowed them whole.

Chapter 36

Echoes of the Past

The storm roared outside, wind whipping through the trees and sending branches clawing at the windows of the Tumblebrook Inn like desperate fingers. Rain poured relentlessly, cascading down the glass in thick, heavy sheets that blurred the world into a dark, swirling haze. The wind howled like a chorus of tormented souls, its eerie wails seeping through the walls and settling into every corner of the inn. Inside, tension was palpable, each room steeped in a suffocating silence that seemed to stretch tighter with each passing second. The inn creaked and groaned as if it, too, felt the weight of what was to come — as though the walls themselves had absorbed decades of secrets and were ready to burst.

Amelia paced the length of the common room, her face pale and drawn, her mind replaying the chaotic escape from the boathouse. Every sound seemed magnified — the creak of a floorboard, the hiss of the wind, the crackle of the fire that spat tiny embers into the air like warnings. Each echo was a reminder they were still vulnerable, still being watched. Every shadow stretched farther, darkening and lengthening, as if the darkness itself was closing in.

The encounter had left them shaken, drenched, and without

answers. Jacob had barricaded the doors, checking and rechecking the locks, his jaw clenched in grim determination. His hands trembled as he adjusted the chair pushed against the door, eyes darting to the windows as though expecting the shadowy figure from the boathouse to reappear at any moment. Clara sat on the couch, a blanket wrapped around her shoulders, eyes distant as she stared at the smoldering embers in the hearth. Lady Grey lay curled at Clara's feet, her fur still damp, eyes half-closed but alert, ears twitching with every creak, tail flicking like a metronome marking time until the next strike.

"We have to go through Nathaniel's notebook again," Amelia said, her voice firm as she tossed the damp, leather-bound journal onto the table. "There's something in here we missed."

"Like what?" Clara asked, her voice hollow, eyes still fixed on the fire. "We already know he was meeting someone that night. But we don't know who — or why."

"Or why he didn't tell us," Millie added, her arms wrapped tightly around herself as if warding off a chill that had settled deep in her bones. "What if Nathaniel was working with the Fixer? What if he was one of them all along?"

"No," Jacob said sharply, turning to face them, jaw tight. "Nathaniel wouldn't do that. He was trying to protect us. He knew something dangerous. That's why he was silenced."

Amelia's expression hardened. "Then what did he know? And why didn't he trust us with it? If he was trying to protect us, why keep us in the dark? Maybe he knew something so dangerous, telling us would've put us in even more danger."

The fire crackled, sparks leaping like tiny embers of rage. Outside, the storm intensified, wind howling as though it carried the voices of the dead. A shiver ran down Clara's spine. The memory of the shadowy figure at the boathouse lingered like a ghostly afterimage.

"What about the notebook?" Clara said, leaning forward, eyes sharpening. "What did Nathaniel write in those last pages? What was he trying to say before... before he vanished?"

Amelia sat down, fingers trembling as she opened the journal. The pages were smeared with water, ink bleeding into paper in dark, inky swirls, but the words remained legible. Each line was a cryptic puzzle — a breadcrumb leading deeper into the labyrinth Nathaniel had tried to escape.

"September 18th," Amelia read aloud. "Meeting confirmed. Boathouse. Midnight. Must bring proof. No going back now."

"Proof?" Millie echoed. "Proof of what?"

"Proof of the Fixer's identity? Or Martin's murder?" Jacob offered.

"Or both," Clara said softly. "Nathaniel was gathering evidence. But he never got the chance to share it."

"Because someone got to him first," Amelia said, closing the journal with a decisive snap. "But we still have the notebook. And we still have each other."

Lady Grey lifted her head, ears pricked, eyes fixed on the window. A low growl rumbled in her throat. The firelight flickered. For a moment, a shadow passed the window — or perhaps it was just the wind stirring the branches. But the feeling of being watched settled heavily over them.

"Did you see that?" Clara whispered.

"We're not alone," Amelia said, voice tight as steel. "And we're running out of time."

Outside, the wind howled — a spectral wail echoing through the night, carrying the ghosts of Tumblebrook's darkest secrets. The storm raged on, but the real storm — the one that had been building for decades — was just beginning to break. Somewhere out there, beneath layers of lies and shadows, the truth waited — a deadly secret ready to rise and drag them all under.

The shadows deepened. The fire guttered low. Every creak felt like a footstep. Every gust of wind like a whisper.

Time was running out.

Chapter 37

The Unmasking

The storm continued to rage outside, a relentless assault of wind and rain that battered the Tumblebrook Inn with unyielding fury. Wind screamed through the trees, bending branches to their breaking points, while rain hammered the roof like a thousand fists pounding in unison. Each gust carried a haunting, mournful howl, as though the very spirits of Tumblebrook were crying out, desperate to be heard.

Inside, the atmosphere was just as tense. Shadows deepened as the fire burned low in the hearth, its dim glow casting restless silhouettes that pulsed and breathed against the walls. The scent of damp wood and burning embers hung in the air, thick with anticipation. Every floorboard creaked like a ghostly footstep, every flicker of flame birthed ominous, shifting shapes.

Amelia stood in the center of the common room, eyes fixed on the small leather-bound notebook Nathaniel had left behind. The pages were stained and smudged, the ink bleeding into the paper in dark, swirling patterns—but the words remained legible, and they told a story that made her blood run cold. The firelight flickered across her face, highlighting the tension carved into her brow and the hard line of her jaw. Her hands trembled slightly as she clutched the notebook.

Clara sat beside her, pale-faced and tense, a blanket draped around her shoulders doing little to stop her shivering. Lady Grey perched on the couch arm, her amber eyes locked on the window, ears twitching with every gust of wind and rain. Jacob stood by the door, jaw clenched and arms crossed, his stance rigid. The room seemed to shrink with each passing second.

"It was all right here," Amelia said, holding up the notebook. "Nathaniel knew. He was going to meet the Fixer at the boathouse."

"And he never came back," Clara whispered. "Because he was silenced."

"But he left this," Amelia said, lifting the notebook. "Everything we need to bring the Fixer down."

"Who was it?" Jacob asked, eyes dark. "Who was he meeting?"

"Someone he trusted," Amelia said grimly. "Someone he thought would help expose the truth."

"And they betrayed him," Clara added, her voice shaking. "They killed him to keep the truth buried."

"We're not letting them get away with it," Amelia said.

"How?" Millie asked from the couch, voice small. "They're powerful. They're watching us."

"We have the names, times, and places," Clara said. "Nathaniel gave us the map. We just need to connect the dots."

"And then what? Go to the police?" Jacob asked. "What if they're in on it?"

"We can't trust anyone yet," Amelia replied. "Not until the proof is undeniable."

"Then we go back to the boathouse," Clara said, rising to her feet. "There's something we missed."

"What if it's a trap?" Millie whispered.

"Then we'll be ready," Amelia said, grabbing her coat. "We're done hiding."

Outside, the wind howled as they stepped into the storm. Rain lashed their faces. Fog pressed around them, heavy with the scent of earth and decay. Every shadow moved. Every gust whispered.

They reached the boathouse, a hulking silhouette in the mist. Its door hung open, creaking. Inside, the scent of mildew and rot clung to the damp air. Floorboards groaned beneath their steps. Lightning flashed, illuminating the warped wood and cobweb-laced rafters.

"There," Clara said, pointing to crates half-submerged in a puddle. "Does that look disturbed? Was this where Nathaniel met the Fixer?."

Amelia moved toward them, flashlight trembling in her grip. The crates were coated in dust, cobwebs stretched like sinister threads. She pried open the top crate.

"Old tools," she muttered. "But they're smeared with..."

"Is that blood?" Jacob asked.

Clara pointed at the floor. "Scratches—like someone was dragged."

The marks led to a trapdoor. Amelia gripped the muddy handle and slipped.

Outside, the storm howled louder. In the distance, unseen but watching, a shadow lingered—eyes gleaming, waiting.

The reckoning had begun.

Chapter 38

The Abyss Below

The trapdoor creaked as it swung open, revealing a yawning chasm of darkness beneath the boathouse floor. The smell hit them first — a cloying stench of wet earth, rotting wood, and something far more ominous. It was thick and suffocating, heavy with the decay of things long buried and secrets long kept. Amelia gripped the flashlight tighter, her knuckles white as she directed the beam into the void. The light barely pierced the blackness, revealing only steep, wooden steps descending into the depths. Each step looked precarious, warped and waterlogged, as though the slightest weight might send them crumbling into the abyss. The air was colder down here, carrying a bone-deep chill that gnawed at their skin.

"Are we really doing this?" Clara asked, her voice wavering. Lady Grey crouched at her feet, amber eyes wide and unblinking, tail twitching nervously. Even the cat seemed to sense the danger that awaited below. Her ears flicked back and forth, attuned to the secrets the darkness kept.

"We have to," Amelia said, her jaw set, eyes dark and determined. "If Nathaniel hid something down there, it might be the only thing that can finally expose the Fixer."

Jacob stepped forward, scanning the trapdoor. "I'll go first. If there's anyone waiting—"

"We all go together," Amelia interrupted, firm. "We don't split up. Not this time."

They exchanged tense glances, then nodded. One by one, they descended. The steps groaned beneath their weight, each creak echoing like a death knell. The walls closed in around them, the wooden planks damp and slimy under their fingertips. The air grew colder with each step, the narrow passage pressing tighter, as though the very space were watching. Each breath fogged before them, vanishing into the oppressive dark.

At the bottom, the passage opened into a cramped, low-ceilinged room. Rotting wooden shelves lined the walls, cluttered with rusted tools, old ropes, and empty glass bottles. The floor was a patchwork of warped boards and muddy earth, puddles of stagnant water gleaming like black mirrors. The air was heavy, and every sound echoed endlessly, as though the room itself swallowed their voices. Somewhere deeper, water dripped steadily, each plop hollow and distant.

"What is this place?" Clara whispered, her breath fogging in the frigid air.

"A storage room," Jacob said cautiously. "But for what?"

"Look," Amelia said, her light landing on a crate shoved against the far wall. "There's something carved into it."

They gathered around the crate. Carved into the wood with a shaky hand: "MARTIN. REMEMBER." The letters were jagged, the wood splintered as though the message had been gouged in desperation.

Clara swallowed hard. "This was his. Martin must have known about this room."

Amelia nodded, heart pounding. "If he hid something, it might still be here."

They pried the crate open. Inside was a tangle of rope, a rusted saw, and a pile of yellowed papers bound with frayed twine. The papers were damp, ink smudged — but legible, a haunting testament to a man unraveling.

Amelia lifted the papers, hands trembling. The top page read:

"They promised me everything. But they took it all away. If I disappear, it wasn't an accident. It was them. It was always them."

Clara sucked in a breath. "Martin knew. He knew they were going to kill him."

"And he tried to leave a record," Jacob said, his eyes darkening. "A confession."

Amelia flipped through the pages. Between two sheets, she found a photograph — grainy, black-and-white. Martin stood beside a man mostly obscured by shadow, but his eyes were unmistakably familiar. Cold. Piercing.

"It's him," Amelia whispered. "The Fixer."

A crash above startled them. The trapdoor slammed shut, the sound reverberating like a gunshot. Darkness engulfed them, the flashlight beam flickering. Footsteps echoed above — slow, deliberate.

"Someone's here," Clara whispered, staring at the ceiling.

Amelia held the light steady, heart racing. The footsteps grew louder. The air pressed tighter, suffocating.

"We're not alone," Jacob said grimly. "They know we're down here."

A shadow passed over the trapdoor. Then silence. For one breathless moment, no one moved. The footsteps resumed, fading into the distance — but the sense of danger remained, wrapping around them like a noose.

They were trapped.

And whoever had sealed them in wasn't finished.

Chapter 39

The Reckoning

The wind continued to howl, slamming against the boathouse with a ferocity that felt almost personal. The wooden walls creaked and groaned under the relentless pressure, as though they, too, bore the weight of the secrets buried beneath them. Inside, the air was thick and stale, laden with the scent of rotting wood and damp earth. The darkness seemed to pulse and breathe, every shadow deepening, every corner feeling as if it harbored unseen eyes. The atmosphere pressed down on them, making the air heavy and suffocating.

Amelia, Clara, and Jacob remained huddled in the darkness, the flashlight flickering weakly as they strained to hear the movements above. The echoes of footsteps still reverberated through the walls, fading like whispers carried on the wind.

"Did they leave?" Clara whispered, her voice taut with fear. Lady Grey's eyes glowed in the dark, her tail twitching as she remained alert, ears perked toward the ceiling. The cat's fur stood on end, her body tense, sensing danger still lingered.

"I don't know," Jacob said, his jaw clenched. "But we can't stay down here forever."

"We need to see what's up there," Amelia said, her voice low and steady. "If they're still watching, we have to know."

They exchanged tense glances, each silently weighing the risk. The trapdoor loomed above like a portal to another world — one that might contain more danger than they could handle. But there was no choice. Slowly, Amelia handed the flashlight to Jacob and placed her hands on the wooden ladder. The wood was slick beneath her palms, and her legs trembled as she began to climb, each rung creaking ominously under her weight. The climb felt endless, every heartbeat loud in her ears.

At the top, she pressed her ear to the trapdoor, listening. Silence. Not a footstep, not a creak. Only the wind and rain pounding the boathouse walls. Swallowing hard, she slowly pushed the trapdoor open just enough to peer through.

Darkness greeted her. The boathouse stood empty, its wide space cast in wavering shadows. Rainwater dripped from the rafters, pooling in dark puddles. The door hung slightly ajar, swinging back and forth with each gust of wind. No sign of the intruder. The shadows twisted into almost-human shapes, dissolving as she blinked.

"It's clear," she whispered, climbing up and holding the trapdoor for Clara and Jacob. They emerged cautiously, eyes scanning for movement.

"Whoever it was, they're gone," Jacob said, moving to the door to peer out into the storm. "But they were definitely here."

"Why slam the trapdoor?" Clara asked, frowning. "Was it a warning?"

"Or a trap," Amelia said, eyes darkening. "They want us to know we're being watched. They're trying to scare us."

Clara knelt beside the trapdoor, studying the floorboards. "Look," she said, tracing muddy footprints leading from the trapdoor to the door. The prints were deep and heavy, as if made by thick boots. The pattern was strange — as though something had been dragged. The mud smeared in long streaks, like a trail.

"What were they carrying?" Jacob muttered, narrowing his eyes. "Or... who?"

A chill raced down Amelia's spine. "Nathaniel," she whispered. "If he was down there..."

"We need to go back," Clara said urgently. "There might be more."

"Or another way out," Amelia added, her mind racing. "If they dragged someone, they might've used a second exit."

Jacob nodded. "Let's go."

They hurried back to the trapdoor, footsteps echoing. Lady Grey darted ahead, ears pricked, eyes sharp, sensing what they couldn't. The air grew colder as they descended, the scent of decay and wet earth thickening. The darkness closed in, the flashlight beam their only guide.

"Look," Clara pointed toward the far wall. "There's a door."

A small, rotting wooden door barely visible behind crates and debris. Jacob braced his shoulder and pushed. The hinges groaned like a scream.

It opened onto a narrow tunnel, its walls braced by bowed beams. The floor was slick with mud, the air ripe with mildew and rot. The tunnel stretched forward into shadows. Amelia stepped forward, her flashlight casting a shivering beam.

"Where does it lead?" Clara asked, her voice shaky.

"Only one way to find out," Amelia said. "But be ready."

Jacob lifted a rusted pipe, jaw set. Clara grabbed a wooden plank, knuckles white. Lady Grey pressed close to Amelia, fur bristling.

They moved in silence, each step echoing through the tunnel like a ticking clock. The air grew colder, thicker. Water dripped steadily, each drop a crash in the silence. A faint light flickered ahead.

"Do you see that?" Clara whispered.

"Someone's there," Amelia said, her pulse pounding. "And they're waiting."

The tunnel widened into a circular chamber. A lantern swung from a hook above, casting eerie shadows. At the center stood a man, his back to them, shoulders hunched, head bowed. A shovel lay at his feet, caked with wet earth. His hands were stained with mud, his clothes torn and soaked.

"Nathaniel?" Amelia whispered.

The man turned. His face was pale, hollow-eyed — but it wasn't Nathaniel.

"You're too late," he rasped. "They took him. And now, they're coming for you."

Chapter 40

The Final Stand

The air in the underground chamber was thick and heavy, saturated with the scent of wet earth and decaying wood. The lantern's weak, wavering light cast long, twisting shadows that seemed to stretch and breathe, as if the very walls were alive and listening. The darkness was oppressive, pressing in from all sides, every echo reverberating through the confined space like a sinister whisper.

The man before them — not Nathaniel — stared with hollow, haunted eyes. His hair clung to his forehead in matted clumps, and his clothes hung from his frame like soaked rags. The shovel at his feet gleamed with damp soil, each muddy droplet falling like blood, pooling in the dirt around his boots.

"Who are you?" Amelia demanded. Her voice echoed, distorted by the chamber's close walls, as if the space were swallowing her words.

The man's lips twisted into a grimace. His eyes darted around the room, hands twitching at his sides. "They took him," he rasped. "Came in the night. Dragged him away. Said he had to be shut up."

"Who?" Clara stepped forward, eyes sharp. "Who took him?"

He glanced toward the tunnel's mouth. "The Fixer's men. Said Nathaniel was asking too many questions."

Amelia's pulse quickened. "Where did they take him? Is he still alive?"

The man flinched. His eyes dropped to the shovel. "The river," he whispered. "Same as Martin. Make it look like an accident."

A chill ran through Clara. The river — the place where Martin's body had been found, where secrets had sunk beneath the current for decades.

"We have to go," Amelia said, jaw set.

As they turned, the man lunged, grabbing Amelia's arm. His grip was bruising. "You can't stop them. They own this town. If you fight them, you're dead."

Jacob stepped in, tearing the man's hand away. "Let her go."

The man stumbled back, chest heaving. "They're everywhere. You can't escape."

"What's your name?" Clara asked, her tone softer. "Maybe we can help each other."

Tears welled in the man's eyes. "I was told to keep quiet. To bury it. But after Martin... after Nathaniel..."

Amelia moved closer. "Tell us."

"They made me bury it," he said. "The ledger. The proof. Under the boathouse. Said if I ever talked..."

"Where exactly?" Jacob pressed.

"Below the floorboards," he said, voice shaking. "They made me dig it. I can still feel the dirt under my nails."

Amelia's heart pounded. "We have to get to the river. Now."

But the man reached out again, his voice urgent. "They're already there. They're waiting for you."

The warning hung heavy. Wind howled through the tunnel, chilling them. Outside, the storm thundered.

Lady Grey pressed close to Amelia, fur on edge. The man's shoulders sagged. He dropped the shovel. Its clang echoed through the room.

"You can't save him," he said, broken. "They're too powerful."

Amelia lifted her chin. Her voice cut through the gloom. "We have to try."

The wind screamed above them, and the river's roar rumbled in the distance — a reminder of the secrets it still held. In the storm's fury, truth waited, hungry to rise, no matter the cost.

Chapter 41

Confrontation and Consequences

The storm outside continued to unleash its fury upon the town of Tumblebrook, the relentless downpour hammering the inn's windows like a thousand accusing fists. Thunder boomed in the distance, its deep, rolling echoes rattling the glass panes. Inside, the inn was a fortress of tension, the air thick and oppressive, weighed down by unspoken fears and simmering rage.

Amelia stood at the center of the room, her damp hair clinging to her forehead, her green eyes blazing with fierce, unyielding determination. The room was dim, lit only by the soft, flickering glow of a single oil lamp, its flame casting long, wavering shadows across the walls.

Clara and Jacob hovered nearby, their expressions tight and wary. Clara's fingers twitched at her sides, her eyes darting between Amelia and the man bound to the chair. Jacob stood with his arms crossed, his jaw clenched, his gaze fixed on the man, his body taut as though ready to spring.

Lady Grey perched on the windowsill, her amber eyes narrowed, her ears pinned back as she watched with predatory intensity. Her tail flicked in slow, deliberate sweeps, a silent metronome marking the passing seconds.

The man they'd dragged from the underground chamber sat slumped in the chair, hands tied behind him, his clothes soaked and muddied, his face gaunt. His wet, matted hair clung to his cheeks, and his glassy eyes stared at the floor, as if wishing to disappear.

"Where is Nathaniel?" Amelia demanded, her voice slicing through the silence.

The man swallowed hard. "You don't understand," he rasped. "They'll come for you. All of you."

"Let them," Clara said, stepping forward. "Not until you tell us what happened."

His gaze flicked toward her, haunted. "They took him to the river. Said he knew too much. Said he had to disappear. Just like Martin."

A chill coiled down Amelia's spine. Always the river. The same place Martin's lifeless body was found years ago. It had swallowed more than just evidence — it had swallowed truth.

"Why the river?" she asked, voice taut. "Why always there?"

He looked away. "Because that's where they bury the truth."

Clara folded her arms. "Who are they?"

"The Fixer and his men. They control everything. The river. The land. The people. You can't fight them."

Amelia met Clara's and Jacob's eyes. "We have to go. Now."

But before they could move, the front door burst open with a thunderous crack. Lady Grey leapt from the sill, fur bristling, eyes locked on the silhouette in the doorway.

"Well, well," said a voice, smooth and dripping malice. "What do we have here?"

Amelia's heart stilled. Royce Harrington stepped inside, rain dripping from his hair, his smile slow and cold.

"You just couldn't leave it alone," Royce said, eyes raking over them. "Had to keep digging."

"Where is Nathaniel?" Amelia asked, voice unsteady.

His smile widened. "Right where he's supposed to be."

"At the river?" Clara asked.

Royce chuckled darkly. "Sharp, Clara. But sharp doesn't mean smart. You think you're close to the truth? You're not."

Amelia stepped forward. "We know about the boathouse. The ledger. The Fixer."

A shadow passed over Royce's face. "You don't know anything. And even if you did, it wouldn't matter. You can't touch him."

"Maybe not," Clara said. "But we can touch you."

Royce's expression tightened. "You don't know what you're getting into. The Fixer isn't a man. He's a ghost. You can't catch a ghost."

"We don't have to," Amelia said. "We just have to catch you."

Royce's eyes flicked around the room, fists clenched. The storm screamed outside, wind and rain pounding the windows. Inside, the tension stretched to its limit.

"This isn't over," Royce growled. And with a turn, he strode out, the door slamming shut behind him.

Amelia exhaled, her shoulders sagging. Lady Grey jumped into her lap, purring steadily against the quiet chaos.

"What now?" Clara asked.

Amelia met her gaze, voice steady. "Now we get to the river. And we find Nathaniel."

Chapter 42

Secrets Beneath the Surface

The rain fell in relentless sheets as Amelia, Clara, and Jacob hurried along the narrow, muddy path leading to the river. The wind whipped through the trees, howling like a chorus of restless spirits. The ground was slick beneath their boots, each step a battle against the sucking mud. Lady Grey weaved between them, her fur plastered to her body, but her amber eyes sharp and alert.

The river loomed ahead — a dark, churning mass surging with the storm's fury. The sound of the rushing water echoed through the trees, a deep, ominous rumble that swallowed all other noise. It was as if the river itself were alive, seething with rage, hungry to claim more secrets.

"This is it," Clara said breathlessly as she reached the riverbank. "This is where they brought him."

Amelia shivered and pulled her coat tighter. The wind bit through the fabric, cutting straight to the bone. "Royce said they took Nathaniel here. If he's still nearby, we have to find him."

Jacob nodded, his expression grim. "We spread out. Look for anything out of place."

Lady Grey bounded ahead, paws silent on the soaked ground.

Her nose twitched, her ears flicking at every noise. The riverbank was strewn with debris — branches, leaves, driftwood — carried down by the swollen current. The river itself was a black, foaming torrent, reflecting flashes of lightning.

Clara knelt beside a cluster of rocks, brushing wet hair from her face as she touched the slick stones. "Here — footprints."

Amelia rushed to her side, her breath fogging in the chill air. The prints were faint and blurred by rain, but they were human. They led straight to the river's edge and vanished into the water.

"They dragged him," Amelia said, heart hammering. "Right to the water."

Jacob stepped closer, frowning. "Did they take him across? Or—"

"Look!" Clara cried, pointing. "By the boathouse."

The old boathouse stood a little way down the bank, its silhouette barely distinguishable against the stormy sky. The doors hung open, creaking in the wind. A lantern flickered inside — pale and unsteady.

"Someone's there," Amelia said. Her stomach flipped. "Nathaniel?"

Without another word, they ran, boots splashing through puddles. Lady Grey shot ahead, tail rigid, ears flattened against the wind.

The howling wind rose to a crescendo as they reached the boathouse. The lantern inside sputtered, casting jerky shadows over the damp wooden walls. The air reeked of mildew and rust.

"Nathaniel?" Amelia called. Her voice echoed. "Are you here?"

For a moment, only silence. Then, a low, muffled sound emerged from the shadows.

"Did you hear that?" Clara whispered. "It's him!"

Amelia's heart leapt. "Nathaniel! We're here!"

They rushed forward, shadows dancing around them. In the far corner, half-buried beneath tarps and ropes, lay Nathaniel. His hands were bound, his soaked clothing clinging to his frail frame. His face was pale, lips cracked, eyes fluttering open.

"Amelia..." he rasped, a ghost of a smile curving his mouth. "You found me."

Amelia dropped to her knees, tearing at the ropes. "We're here now. You're safe."

Nathaniel winced as the bonds fell away. "They... were going to—"

"You don't need to talk," Clara said gently. "Rest."

But Nathaniel shook his head, panic flashing in his eyes. "The ledger," he gasped. "They threw it in the river."

Amelia froze. "The river?"

He nodded toward the door. "They said no one would ever find it."

Lady Grey growled low, ears pinned, gaze fixed on the door. A gust of wind extinguished the lantern, plunging them into darkness.

"We need to move," Jacob said sharply. "Now."

Supporting Nathaniel, Amelia helped him to his feet, his arm slung over her shoulder. They stepped into the storm just as lightning lit the sky — and there, caught in the raging current, floated a wooden crate. Its lid was ajar, its contents spilling into the river. Pages fluttered like dying birds, ink bleeding away.

"The ledger," Clara breathed.

Amelia held Nathaniel close as he sagged against her. "I'm sorry," he whispered. "I tried."

Amelia's eyes flared with resolve. "It's not over. Not yet."

Lady Grey pressed against her side, amber eyes fixed on the river. In the distance, dark figures loomed in the shadows, watching. Waiting. And in the river, the truth slipped further from reach, one sodden page at a time.

Chapter 43

Unmasking the Fixer

The air inside the inn was thick with the scent of wet earth and river water, a lingering reminder of their frantic search along the riverbank. Amelia and Clara helped Nathaniel onto the worn leather sofa, draping a quilt over his shoulders as he shivered, his skin pale and clammy. Lady Grey leapt onto the arm of the sofa, her amber eyes fixed on Nathaniel, her tail swishing in a slow, rhythmic arc.

"He's burning up," Clara said, pressing the back of her hand to Nathaniel's forehead. "We need to get him warm."

Amelia nodded, her jaw clenched as she tossed another log onto the fire. The flames crackled and hissed, casting flickering shadows across the walls. The room was dim, lit only by the fire and a single lamp on the side table. Outside, the storm hadn't relented — rain still lashed the windows like a thousand tiny daggers.

"Nathaniel," Amelia said, kneeling beside him. "Can you hear me?"

Nathaniel's eyelids fluttered, his eyes glassy and unfocused. "Amelia..." he whispered, his voice thin. "They were going to... the river..."

"We know," Amelia said gently. "You're safe now. But we need to know — is the ledger really gone?"

Nathaniel's eyes filled with tears, his chest rising and falling in uneven breaths. "They threw it in the water," he said, his voice cracking. "Said no one would ever find it. But..."

"But what?" Clara leaned forward. "What did they say?"

"The Fixer..." Nathaniel's voice trembled, his gaze darting around the room as though expecting the Fixer to appear. "He said... it doesn't matter if the ledger's found. He's already destroyed the real evidence."

Amelia's heart sank. "The real evidence?"

Nathaniel nodded urgently. "The ledger was just a decoy. The real evidence is in the old tannery. Records... documents... everything."

Clara's breath caught. "The tannery? But that place has been abandoned for years."

"Exactly," Nathaniel said. "No one would think to look there. But it's all there — the ledgers, the contracts, the bribes. Everything the Fixer's been hiding."

Amelia met Clara's gaze, her jaw set. "Then we go to the tannery."

Nathaniel's hand shot out, gripping Amelia's wrist. "No," he said, his eyes wide. "He'll know. He always knows."

"We don't have a choice," Amelia said. "If we don't act now, he'll cover his tracks for good."

Nathaniel's grip loosened, exhaustion overtaking him. "Be careful... he's always watching..."

Lady Grey let out a low, mournful meow. Amelia's heart pounded. They'd been behind the Fixer for too long. If they didn't act now, they might lose their only chance.

"We have to move quickly," Clara said, grabbing her coat. "If the tannery's where the real evidence is, we need to get there before he clears it out."

Amelia nodded, lacing her boots. "Jacob," she said, turning. "Stay here with Nathaniel. Lock the doors. Don't let anyone in."

Jacob nodded grimly. "Be careful."

"We will," Amelia said.

Lady Grey trotted to the door, tail high, ready. The wind howled, rattling the windows. But it wasn't the storm that chilled Amelia — it was the secrets waiting at the tannery.

The tannery loomed dark against the turbulent sky. Its shattered windows gaped like eye sockets. The scent of wet earth and rotting wood hung in the air. Each step squelched through mud. The building creaked and groaned, its rusted skeleton groaning in protest.

Amelia and Clara moved cautiously, scanning the shadows. The tannery was a maze of broken beams and rusted machinery. Wind whistled through the broken windows like a dying breath.

"Do you hear that?" Clara whispered. "Footsteps."

Amelia held her breath. Crunching gravel. They ducked behind crates. Lady Grey crouched low, ears flattened.

A figure entered — tall, hooded, deliberate. The Fixer.

"I told you not to get involved," he said, voice smooth with menace. "But you couldn't help yourselves."

Amelia stepped forward. "We know what you did to Martin. And to Nathaniel. It ends here."

The Fixer chuckled, hollow. "This town is mine. Every deal. Every secret."

"You've ruined lives," Clara said. "It's all coming out."

The Fixer stepped closer. "You're brave, Clara. But bravery isn't enough."

"And fear doesn't last," Amelia replied. "Your time is up."

The Fixer's jaw clenched.

"We know who you are," Clara said, holding up papers. "Signed ledgers. Your deals. Your name."

Lady Grey growled. The Fixer stepped forward — and froze in a blaze of flashlight beams.

"Freeze!" a voice shouted.

Police burst through the tannery. Radios crackled. Guns raised.

Amelia exhaled, watching as the Fixer was cuffed and led away. Lady Grey rubbed against Clara, purring low.

But Amelia couldn't shake the feeling: the river still held secrets. Ones that refused to stay buried.

Chapter 44

The Aftermath

The dawn broke over Tumblebrook with a tentative, golden glow, the storm clouds finally dispersing to reveal a soft, misty morning. The air was rich with the scent of wet earth and fallen leaves, and the river, once a raging torrent, now flowed gently beneath the delicate light. Despite the calm, the atmosphere inside the inn remained tense, a quiet weight pressing down on everyone gathered within.

Amelia stood in the parlor, her hands wrapped around a steaming cup of tea, her eyes fixed on the window as she watched the mist roll over the hills. Lady Grey perched beside her, amber eyes sharp, scanning the horizon as if still searching for shadows from the night before.

"I still can't believe it," Clara said, her voice soft and weary as she settled into the armchair. "The Fixer... all this time. Right under our noses."

Amelia nodded, her jaw tight. "It's not over. They may have taken him into custody, but he wasn't working alone. There are still people out there—those who helped him, those who profited from his silence."

Clara drew her knees up, wrapping her arms around them. "And the ledger... it's still out there somewhere."

"We'll find it," Amelia said firmly. "We have to."

Before Clara could respond, the door creaked open and Jacob entered, his expression grim. "Nathaniel's awake. He's asking for you."

Amelia set her cup aside and rose. Clara followed her down the hallway to the guest room, where Nathaniel lay propped up by pillows, pale but alert.

"Amelia," he rasped. "Clara."

Clara pulled a chair close. "How are you feeling?"

Nathaniel gave a faint smile. "Like I've been hit by a train. But I remember everything."

Amelia leaned closer. "What do you remember?"

His face turned serious. "The ledger. The real one. It was never in the river. That was just to throw everyone off."

Clara's eyes widened. "Then where is it?"

"Before they took me to the river, they brought me to the old general store. They kept me in the basement. I saw them bring in a crate—heavy, locked, and marked with the same emblem from Martin's journal."

Amelia frowned. "The Harrington family crest."

"Exactly. That's where the ledger is. They hoped we'd keep searching the river while they cleared out the real evidence."

Amelia and Clara exchanged a look. Determination flared in their eyes.

"Then we go," Amelia said.

Jacob stepped forward. "Not without me."

"Together," Clara agreed.

Nathaniel gripped Amelia's hand. "Be careful. If they find out..."

"They won't," Amelia said. "We're ending this."

* * *

The old general store loomed before them, its wood siding warped, the sign above the door askew and unreadable. A gust of wind stirred the mist curling through the street.

"This place gives me the creeps," Clara murmured, clutching her coat.

"Stay close," Jacob said, eyes sweeping the shadows.

Amelia pushed the door open. Hinges groaned. Inside, the air was musty and cold, the room littered with empty shelves and crates. The floor creaked underfoot.

"Nathaniel said basement," Clara whispered.

"Here," Lady Grey meowed, her tail flicking toward a door behind the counter.

The staircase beyond descended into darkness. Jacob led the way, flashlight cutting through the gloom. The basement was damp, lined with shelves stacked high with crates, many marked with the Harrington crest.

"There," Clara said, pointing to a locked crate.

Amelia knelt beside it, brushing dust from the rusted lock.

"Stand back," Jacob said, wedging a crowbar into place.

The lock snapped open. Inside, musty air billowed out, revealing stacks of leather-bound ledgers. Amelia opened one, scanning the pages.

"It's all here—bribes, land deals, payments. Everything."

Clara pulled out a notebook. "Martin's name. He was trying to expose it all."

A creak echoed above them.

"Someone's coming," Jacob whispered.

Amelia stuffed the ledger into her bag. "Let's move."

They slipped back upstairs, the store silent but oppressive. Outside, the mist swallowed the street. Still, every shadow felt watchful.

The river had hidden lies. But the general store held the truth.

Now they had to survive long enough to tell it.

Chapter 45

Breaking the Silence

The sky above Tumblebrook was a dull, muted gray, the kind that held the promise of more rain. The air was thick and heavy, charged with a foreboding that clung to every corner of the town. Inside the inn, tension simmered as Amelia, Clara, and Jacob gathered around the dining table, the ledger and notebooks spread out before them like pieces of a complex, sinister puzzle.

Amelia's green eyes were steely, her jaw tight as she flipped through the ledger's pages, scanning line after line of incriminating evidence. Each entry was a damning thread in the Fixer's web — bribes to officials, hush money to silence dissent, illicit land deeds. Everything they needed to expose the entire operation lay before them in black and white.

"It's worse than we thought," Amelia said, her voice taut. "The Harringtons paid off police, council members, even logging crews. And look — these payments marked with just initials. The Fixer's fingerprints."

Clara leaned in, brow furrowed. "Who else knows about this?"

"Too many," Jacob replied grimly. "If we go public now, we're not just exposing the Harringtons. We're putting ourselves in the crosshairs."

Amelia's fists clenched. "We can't sit on this. We have to go to the police."

"And risk handing it to someone already bought?" Clara asked. "What if the Fixer has insiders? He could erase everything overnight."

Amelia's mind raced. Trust was scarce in Tumblebrook. The town had been hollowed out by fear and silence. They needed a way to blow the doors off — clean and loud.

"We need someone we can trust," Amelia said finally, glancing at Jacob. "Outside of town. Someone who can get this to the right people."

Jacob nodded. "I have a friend in Duluth. A reporter. If I get this to her, she'll publish everything. Once it's out, they can't bury it."

Clara glanced at the window. "But how do we get it out without being seen? The Fixer's eyes are everywhere."

"We need a diversion," Amelia said. "Something to keep them occupied while Jacob makes his move."

Clara's eyes lit up. "The town square meeting. It's today. Everyone will be there — the Harringtons, their lackeys."

"Perfect," Jacob said. "We confront them publicly. While they're distracted, I disappear."

Amelia's jaw tightened. "We'll have to make a scene. Big enough to shake the whole square."

Clara nodded grimly. "And it means putting ourselves directly in their path."

Amelia took a breath. No more hiding. No more shadows.

Lady Grey leapt onto the table, her amber eyes fixed on the ledger. Her tail flicked, a silent warning. The time had come.

"Let's do this," Amelia said.

* * *

The town square brimmed with people. Under the sullen sky, murmurs buzzed through the crowd like static. The Harringtons' platform stood in the center — all polished wood and false promises.

Amelia and Clara stood near the fringe, scanning the sea of faces. Jacob was already gone, the ledger hidden in his coat, his path winding through back alleys toward safety.

"Ready?" Clara asked.

Amelia nodded. "Let's make some noise."

The crowd hushed as Royce Harrington stepped up to the microphone, wearing his usual mask of practiced charm.

"Thank you for being here," he began, voice smooth as oil. "I want to address some recent rumors about my family."

Amelia stepped forward, her voice ringing out. "You mean the rumors about bribes? Buried bodies? Ledgers full of blood money?"

Gasps rippled through the crowd. Royce's face froze.

"Amelia Farnsworth," he said coolly. "I don't know what you're implying."

"You know exactly what I'm saying," Amelia shot back. "You've been bleeding this town for years. It ends now."

Clara stepped up. "Martin tried to expose you. You silenced him. Nathaniel, too. But he survived. And we have the truth."

Royce's smile curdled. "You have no proof."

"We do," Amelia said. "And it's already on its way to someone who can expose you."

Confusion stirred the crowd. Royce's fists clenched.

"You don't know what you're doing," he growled. "You're playing with fire."

"Then let's burn it all down," Clara replied.

Wind gusted through the square. Raindrops began to fall. Lady Grey let out a low growl, eyes fixed on figures weaving through the crowd — men in hats, collars high.

"They're here," Amelia whispered.

"Then we hold the line," Clara said.

Amelia faced Royce. "It's over. The whole town is watching."

And as the rain came down, the tension shattered. Townsfolk murmured, turning to one another. Doubt rippled like thunder.

Whatever came next, the silence was broken — and Tumblebrook would never be the same.

Epilogue

New Beginnings

The summer sun bathed Tumblebrook in a warm, golden glow, the sky a brilliant expanse of blue stretched above the town like a fresh canvas. The air was fragrant with wildflowers and freshly cut grass—a stark contrast to the storm-laden days that had finally surrendered to peace. The river flowed gently now, its once-turbulent depths smooth and reflective beneath the soft light, as if washing away the last of the town's buried shadows.

Amelia Farnsworth stood on the wraparound porch of the inn, a steaming cup of coffee cradled in her hands. Beneath her bare feet, the wooden planks were warm from the sun, and from inside drifted the hum of voices, the clatter of teacups, and the occasional burst of laughter—music she had missed more than she'd realized. The inn was alive again. Truly alive. And so, in many ways, was she.

Inside, Clara was arranging a vase of fresh daisies and sunflowers in the foyer, while the scent of cinnamon and vanilla curled from the kitchen. No alarms. No whispers. No fear creeping around corners.

"Can't believe how much has changed," Clara said, stepping out onto the porch beside her. Her eyes were soft with wonder. "It feels like the whole town is waking up after a long, dark sleep."

Amelia smiled, her green eyes misting. "It's more than that," she said quietly. "It's like we finally remembered who we are."

They stood in silence for a moment, shoulder to shoulder, letting the sunlight settle on their skin. Across the square, the townspeople gathered near a new bronze plaque mounted beside the town hall steps. Names gleamed in the morning light—Martin Hale, Nathaniel Harrington, Eleanor Perkins, and others who had dared to speak the truth, to stand in the light even when it cost them everything.

"It's strange," Clara said softly. "How grief and healing can live side by side. Like this town—so full of wounds, but now... blooming."

Amelia's throat tightened. She looked at the plaque again, then at the river that wound peacefully through the hills beyond. "They deserve to be remembered," she said. "And so do the people still here —the ones who stayed, who chose to keep going."

Clara nodded, then smiled. "Did you hear? Millie's hosting a book signing next week. At Gossamer Fables. She's calling her memoir *Scones and Scandals*."

Amelia laughed, a real, unguarded laugh that startled even herself. "Of course she is."

"And she's donating half the proceeds to renovating the town library," Clara added, her eyes twinkling.

"That's Millie for you," Amelia said, her voice warm. "Always keeping the story going."

Lady Grey trotted toward them then, her silver-tipped fur gleaming in the sun. She brushed gently against Amelia's leg before leaping onto the porch railing, amber eyes fixed on the river in a way that made Amelia shiver—part reverence, part vigilance.

"You always knew, didn't you?" Amelia murmured, scratching behind the cat's ears. "You saw it all before we did."

Lady Grey blinked slowly, as if to say, *Of course. Someone had to keep watch.*

"What about you?" Clara asked gently. "What now?"

Amelia turned to her, the question lingering. For so long, her life had been about preservation—of the inn, of her memories, of her place in a town haunted by its silence. Now the silence had been broken. Now there was space for something new.

"I don't know yet," Amelia admitted, her voice thick. "But for the first time, I'm not afraid to find out."

She looked down at her hands, still wrapped around the warm mug, and then out across the town. The windows of the café were open. Children's laughter echoed faintly from the park. And in the distance, the church bells rang—not solemnly, but like a call to begin again.

"Now we rebuild," Amelia said. "The inn. The town. Ourselves."

Clara slipped her arm through Amelia's and leaned into her side. "Together?"

Amelia met her gaze, her heart swelling. "Together."

The sun rose higher, spilling gold across the hills, and with it came a sense of quiet absolution. Tumblebrook had suffered. It had fractured. But it had endured. And as the light touched the riverbank and brushed the rooftops, the town—its people, its history, and its future—stood whole again.

From her perch, Lady Grey flicked her tail and gave a soft, approving chirp. The past, for now, could rest.

The future was calling.

And this time, Amelia was ready to answer.